BOOK THREE

Friends Forever?

Read all the Mackenzie Blue books

MACKENZIE BLUE

MACKENZIE BLUE #2: THE SECRET CRUSH

MACKENZIE BLUE #3: FRIENDS FOREVER?

BOOK THREE
Friends Forever?

By
Tina Wells

Illustrations by Michael Segawa

HARPER
An Imprint of HarperCollins*Publishers*

Library of Congress Cataloging-in-Publication Data is available.
ISBN 978-0-06-158314-8

Typography by Alison Klapthor

10 11 12 13 14   LP/RRDB   10 9 8 7 6 5 4 3 2 1
❖
First Edition

For Phoebe Moragne Washington

1
Camp Week

Adam Carmichael pulled his subcompact car into Jasper Chapman's driveway and turned to his sister, Mackenzie Blue. "Go get Jasper, Zee," he told her.

"I would if I could move," Zee said, pointing to the giant red backpack that was sitting on her lap and nearly touched the car's ceiling.

"I can get Jasper!" Chloe Lawrence-Johnson called from the backseat. "My luggage is in the trunk." She opened the back door and hurried up the walk to Jasper's front door, her ponytail bouncing with each step.

"How come Zee and I have to ride with our luggage smothering us, and Chloe gets to put hers in the trunk?" Ally Stern, who was also sitting in the back, asked.

"Well . . . ," Adam began, pretending that he was giving the question serious consideration. "Maybe it's because Zee has another bag *and* her guitar back there. My trunk could barely fit all that." He picked up his iPhone and began typing a text message.

Zee twisted in her seat just enough to see Ally roll her eyes. "It's not my fault you drive such a little car," Ally said.

"If you would prefer to walk the rest of the way, be my guest," Adam told her without pausing from his text message.

"Sorry, Ally," Zee apologized to her BFF. Ally had moved to France the previous summer. But now, she was staying with Zee for two weeks while her journalist parents traveled for work. A former Brookdale Academy student, Ally was joining the others on the annual seventh-grade field trip to Brookdale Mountain.

Chloe returned with Jasper, who had his bass and the smallest overnight bag Zee had ever seen.

"Oh my gosh, Jasper!" Ally gasped as the friends got back in the car. "Did you bring enough for the whole week?" she asked.

"I don't really need more than a toothbrush and some clothes," Jasper told her. "Besides, the key to proper packing is how you fold—or should I say, roll—your clothes."

"*Roll* your clothes?" Zee asked.

Jasper nodded. "You can fit more—and you avoid wrinkles," he explained in his British accent. Jasper had moved from London over the summer.

Zee examined the luggage on her lap. "*Now* you tell me."

"This trip is going to be sooo awesome!" Chloe exclaimed as Adam put down his iPhone and began to back out of the driveway. "Isn't it, Zee?"

"Sure." Zee paused. "If you think roughing it in the middle of nowhere is fun."

"I do," Chloe said, smiling. Her southern accent always sounded a little stronger when she was excited. "I hope we see tons of animals. On Brookdale Mountain, there are raccoons, skunks, coyotes—even mountain lions!"

"Mountain lions?" Zee's eyes grew. "As in predators with

huge, sharp claws and teeth?"

Chloe laughed. "Don't worry. We'll be lucky if we see one."

"Lucky?" Zee said.

"Please tell me that's a joke," Ally said.

"It's not a joke," Chloe said. "But it's really not a big deal. Wild animals are afraid of humans."

"I just hope *they* remember that," Zee replied. She smoothed her red bangs under her blue headband.

"Well, I'll be happy to see some of your American skunks," Jasper added.

"*I* won't!" Zee said. "The bug bites and outdoor toilets were already creeping me out. Now you guys are making this trip sound even worse."

Adam rounded the corner into the school parking lot. "It's too late to turn back now," Adam told her. "We're here."

"Maybe I'll just say I couldn't make it because I was stuck under my luggage," Zee mumbled.

Chloe giggled. "I'll come pull it off you," she said, heading around the car to help Zee, as Jasper and Ally got out, too. Chloe pointed to Adam, who was still behind the wheel, back to typing on his iPhone. "I'm surprised Adam drove us," she said. "I thought your parents were going to."

"They were—until my mother started crying while we were eating breakfast," Zee said. "I'd have been mortified if she'd stood in the parking lot, bawling."

"Because you'd end up crying, too?" Chloe asked.

"Exactly," Zee said. "I'm really going to miss my parents. I've never been away from them for as long as five days."

"I've gone to sleepaway camp for the past three summers, so my parents were fine," Chloe said. "In fact, compared to six weeks of summer camp, this is pretty much nothing."

"What about your parents, Jasper?" Ally asked.

Jasper held up his bag. "Guess what's in here besides clothes?"

The girls shrugged.

"Sunscreen," Jasper explained. "*Five* bottles."

"No way!" Zee's mouth hung open.

"My mom woke me up in the middle of the night to remind me to put it on—even when I'm in the woods."

"Well . . . you do have light skin," Ally pointed out.

"*Nobody* needs a bottle of sunscreen per day," Jasper protested.

"I guess she's a little nervous about you going away," Chloe said.

"Yes," Jasper agreed. "Quite."

"I think you guys are lucky," Ally told them. "With my parents' crazy schedule, I never know when I'll even get to talk to them."

"Aww," Chloe said sympathetically.

"But Ginny and J.P. are like my second parents," Ally continued, "so it's almost as good to have them worrying about me."

"I can't believe you call Zee's parents by their first names," Chloe said.

Ally shrugged.

Adam emerged from the driver's seat of his car.

"What took you so long?" Zee asked.

"I was tweeting," Adam explained.

"Tweeting?" Jasper asked.

"You know . . . Twitter," Zee prompted. "As if the world would fall apart if everybody didn't know what Adam was doing all the time."

"There's a way to find out what Adam—I mean, some-one—is doing every moment?" Chloe asked, her eyes growing round.

"Drool alert!" Zee whispered to Chloe, but if Adam

caught on to the fact that Chloe had a crush on him, he didn't let on.

"It'll be great to get some fresh air and commune with nature, huh, guys?" Adam said, looking right at Zee. He sucked in deeply as if he were standing on the top of Brookdale Mountain.

Zee had lived long enough with her seventeen-year-old brother to know she was being taunted. "How about you commune with nature, and I'll stay home in my comfortable bed?"

"Uh . . . how about no," Adam countered. "I already went on the Brookdale Mountain field trip when I was in seventh grade. Your turn."

"We'll just be gone until Friday," Chloe reminded Zee.

"That's five whole days," Adam repeated. "It should give me enough time to convert the twins' bedroom into a sauna." He called Ally and Zee "the twins" because before Ally moved, they were practically inseparable. Sometimes they even dressed alike. That day Zee and Ally both had on cargo shorts and similar purple T-shirts.

"Very funny," Zee said sarcastically to Adam, even though everyone really was laughing. "If even one piece of paper is out of place . . . ," she threatened.

"And how would you be able to tell?" Adam asked.

Zee paused. Her room was usually a disorganized mess.

Suddenly, a shout rang across the parking lot. "Everyone, it's time to board the bus!" Ms. Merriweather, Brookdale Academy's seventh-grade science teacher was gathering students together.

Zee looked at her friends. "Let's go!" Maybe the science trip wouldn't be so bad. After all, she'd be missing a week of school and hanging out with her best friends in the world.

Zee, Ally, Jasper, and Chloe placed their luggage on the heap with the rest of the seventh graders' bags. As they walked toward the bus steps, they were joined by the rest of the boys in their fifth-period science class: Marcus Montgomery, Conrad Mitori, and Landon Beck—*the* cutest boy at Brookdale Academy.

All the boys got on the bus, but Adam grabbed Zee's shoulder. "Wait!" he said.

"What?" Zee asked. Ally and Chloe turned toward him, too.

"Watch out for the Mountain Man," Adam warned.

"Oh, please," Ally said, snorting.

When Adam's serious expression didn't change, Zee said, "The Mountain Man?"

"He lives on Brookdale Mountain. . . ." Adam stopped

and shook his head. "Never mind. Maybe he won't bother you."

"Probably not," Ally said, "since he doesn't exist."

"Who's the Mountain Man?" Chloe asked.

Adam wore a faraway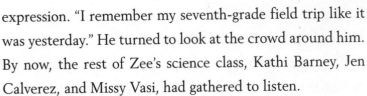
expression. "I remember my seventh-grade field trip like it was yesterday." He turned to look at the crowd around him. By now, the rest of Zee's science class, Kathi Barney, Jen Calverez, and Missy Vasi, had gathered to listen.

"What happened?" Zee asked.

"Someone—or should I say, some*thing*—lived on the mountain."

"Wasn't he human?" Chloe wondered.

"Well," Adam began, "he walked upright and wore human clothes, but he had hair all over his body."

"Ewww!" Kathi exclaimed. "Even on his back?"

Adam nodded. "Everywhere. Legend has it that he can't speak, so he grunts. There's only one phrase he says."

"What?" Chloe whispered, mesmerized.

"I . . . want . . . my . . . leg . . . back."

"He's missing a leg? How does he walk?" Ally asked suspiciously.

"He uses a crutch," Adam answered immediately.

As Zee's stomach twisted with fear, she wished she could be more like Ally. Zee was already nervous about being away from her parents for five days, and Adam was not helping.

"He limps down from the mountain every year during the field trip," Adam continued.

"Really?" Kathi asked. "I've never heard that, and I know a lot of eighth graders—one in particular."

Zee knew Kathi wanted everyone to ask what she meant by "one in particular," but Adam barreled ahead. "Even if no one actually sees him," he told her, "there's usually evidence that he's been near the cabins."

Marcus stuck his face through the open bus window above their heads. "Hey!" he shouted at the girls. "It's time to go!"

Ally grabbed Zee's arm. "C'mon. Marcus is right," Ally said, guiding Zee up the bus steps.

"Bye-o-nara," Adam called out.

"I'll make sure all your luggage gets on the bus. 'Cause that's just the kind of guy I am."

"Thanks, big bro!" Zee shouted behind her.

"See you on Friday," Ally added.

The other fifth-period science girls boarded behind Zee and Ally.

As Zee walked down the long aisle to a seat in the back, she noticed Marcus and Jasper huddled with Landon and Conrad. They stopped whispering and sat up straight as the girls moved past.

Landon glanced at Zee and smiled. *Don't blush. Don't blush. Don't blush,* she silently pleaded—as her face got hotter and hotter. Zee had had a crush on Landon since forever. But they'd recently decided to be just friends. She grinned at Landon, then quickly sat down beside Chloe in the row of seats behind the group. Ally sat on the other side of her.

Kathi, Jen, and Missy filled in the row behind them as Mr. P moved down the aisle. His name was short for Mr. Papademetriou, and he was Zee's favorite teacher and the director of her band, the Beans. The fifth-period science students were all members.

"Oh, good," he said. "You're all together. I know some of you brought your instruments, which is really cool, because there should be plenty of free time for you guys to get together for jam sessions."

"What's a jam session?" Conrad asked.

"You know, when you just hang out and play and sing together for fun," Mr. P explained.

"Cool beans!" Zee said. Then she called out, "Mr. P, just so you know, Ally brought her flute."

"That's great." Mr. P smiled at Ally. "You can be an honorary member of the Beans."

"Thanks!" Ally said. "That's so awesome!"

"The instruments will be kept in the main lodge," Mr. P continued.

"Will they be safe?" Kathi asked. "My violin is worth *a lot* of money."

Chloe rolled her eyes and Zee stifled a giggle.

"Yes, they'll be locked up when no one is in the lodge," Mr. P said.

The bus driver closed the door and started the engine, so Mr. P scrambled for a seat in the front with Ms. Merriweather and the chaperones.

As the bus pulled away, all of the students cheered. Zee pulled out her diary and began writing.

Hi, Diary,

I hope I can survive for five days and four nights away from my parents. (I'm already feeling a little homesick. ☹) But it's also five days with Landon. ☺ And Ally. ☺ ☺ I wish I could be more like her. She's staying with us for two weeks, and her parents are thousands of miles away. She's not freaked out about it at all.

I think I just need to figure out the good stuff and the bad stuff about this week—then focus on the good stuff.

Zee

Good Stuff	Bad Stuff
• Getting to be with Ally, Chloe, and Jasper.	• Missing my parents.
	• Having to walk around sweaty and gross in front of Landon.
• Getting to be with Landon!!!!!!	
• No school uniforms!	• Mountain lions, bears, and skunks.

Good Stuff (continued)	Bad Stuff (continued)
• No homework for a week.	• Bathrooms and showers made out of wood. (Splinters!)
• No Adam for a week.	• No Adam for a week. (Don't tell him I said that.)
• No lunchroom food.	
• The talent show!!	• Camp food.
	• Living without my laptop, Wii, and TV.

P.S. Ally grew boobs in France! Plus, she has a boyfriend—Jacques. I'm getting left in the dust. (But I know she would never really leave me behind. Zee + Ally = BFF!)

Zee closed her diary and dropped it in the tote bag she'd made out of a tank top. Then she turned toward Ally, who was leaning over the seat in front of them, chatting with Jasper.

"What are you guys talking about?" Zee asked.

"I was giving Ally a guide to London," Jasper said.

"Oh yeah," Zee said. "I really want to visit the Tower of London. All of those terrible kings and queens lived there and did all those horrible things."

Ally sat back in her seat. "That's definitely cool, but we're not talking about touristy places." As she shook her head, her long brown hair brushed her shoulders. "Jasper's giving me insider tips on the best shopping, secret bakeries, great tea . . ."

"I don't think I could ever trade my Frappuccinos for tea," Zee said.

"That's because you've never had real English tea." Ally leaned forward again.

"Maybe," Zee said. She looked at Chloe, who was staring out the window. "Want to make friendship bracelets?" Zee asked her. Without waiting for an answer, she pulled bundles of red, blue, and purple string out of her bag. She placed a container of wooden beads on the seat between them.

"I found out how to make really awesome chunky ones," Chloe said as she began braiding. "I'm gonna make the first one for you!"

"Thanks," Zee said, slowly turning to look from Chloe to Ally. She wasn't sure who she'd make her first bracelet for.

2

Check-in

As the camp bus climbed the narrow, curving dirt road, each bump and jolt reminded Zee how far away from civilization she was. Finally, a sign rose in the distance.

BROOKDALE MOUNTAIN CAMPGROUNDS

The bus turned onto an even narrower, curvier path, then finally stopped and opened its door.

Students unbuckled seat belts and scrambled into the aisle. Mr. P stood up at the front. "Everyone, grab your luggage from the last bus and wait for more instructions," he announced. Then he hurried down the bus steps before the herd of rushing seventh graders.

After the bus driver unloaded the luggage, Zee pointed to her backpack. "Could you guys help me with this?" she asked her friends.

"Sure," Chloe said. She and Ally struggled to get the bag off the ground. The two girls managed to lift it high enough for Zee to reach her arms through the straps. Zee leaned over slightly to balance the heavy pack on her body.

"Did you bring your entire closet?" Jasper asked.

"No way," Zee said. She reached down and pulled out the handle of a small matching suitcase on rollers. "It wouldn't all fit in both of these."

Ally looked at Jasper. "Her mother wouldn't let her take

a third bag," she explained.

"Why did you bring so much?" Jasper asked Zee.

"How can I know what I'm going to want to wear a week ahead of time?" Zee said. "What if I change my mind?"

"I suppose that would be quite disastrous," Jasper said.

Zee eyed him suspiciously. "Are you being sarcastic?"

Kathi joined the group and saved Jasper from having to answer. She scrunched up her nose and sniffed. "What's that smell?"

"Yeah," Jen agreed. "It's really weird."

Zee, Ally, Jasper, and Chloe inhaled deeply.

"Does it smell like trees?" Zee asked.

"Yes!" Kathi responded.

"I think that's nature," Chloe spoke slowly.

"Well, I hope it goes away," Kathi said.

"Ow!" Zee said, slapping her leg.

"Why are you hitting yourself?" Ally asked.

"A mosquito bit me."

"Oh my gosh!" Kathi yelled. "I better hide. Mosquitoes loooove me."

"Maybe that's because you both make an annoying, high-pitched noise," Ally mumbled.

Kathi looked around frantically. "When do we get to go to the hotel, Mr. P?" she called out, pointing to a huge stone-and-log building in the distance.

"That's the main lodge, for indoor activities and meetings," Mr. P said. He pointed into the woods in the opposite direction—to ten small wooden shacks with screens in the windows. "We'll sleep in the cabins."

"Mr. P!" Kathi shouted, hurrying toward their teacher. "Do my parents know about this?"

"Probably." Mr. P stuck a pencil behind his ear and flipped through the papers on his clipboard. "Since you're in science and the band together, the Beans will be in cabins one and two—girls in one, and boys in two. You all can head over and get settled. Meet me at the lodge in fifteen minutes."

As Mr. P read the assignments for the rest of the campers, Zee and the others walked toward their cabins. Zee quickly realized that rolling suitcases didn't work very well on dirt paths. To make matters worse, under the weight of her heavy backpack, she couldn't keep her balance. First, she veered off to the left. Then to the right. Then she stumbled backward. Right into Landon!

Landon steadied Zee by wrapping both of his arms around her. She was certain that he must have been able to feel her heart thumping.

"Oh, uh, thanks," Zee said.

Landon pulled away quickly. "Are you okay now?" Even with his surfer's tan, Zee could see that Landon was blushing beneath the blond bangs that hung slightly over his face.

Zee avoided looking directly into his amazingly blue eyes. She was afraid she'd say something like, "I am now" or "Yes, thanks to you." Yuck!

"Yeah . . . I'm . . . uh . . . fine. Totally." Zee stumbled a little more but managed to stay upright without any help.

When Landon saw that Zee was okay, he rushed to catch up with Marcus and Conrad.

Jasper hurried to Zee's side, his own olive-green nylon pack perfectly square on his back. "Why don't I take your rolling luggage?" he asked, grabbing the handle.

"Thanks!" Zee said.

"That's very gentlemanly of you, Jasper," Ally said.

"Well, I like to think it's what anyone would do." Jasper looked in Landon's direction. "Although perhaps I'm wrong."

Ally moved nearer to Zee. "So did you do that on purpose to get Landon to notice you?"

"No!" Zee and Jasper said at the same time.

Zee, Ally, and Chloe stared at Jasper.

"I mean," Jasper quickly added, "that's not exactly the best way to get a guy's attention."

"Ohhh?" Ally asked curiously. "Maybe you should tell us what *is* the best way."

Jasper gulped and looked down at the ground.

"I'm just kidding," Ally said with a flick of her hand.

"Besides, Zee and Landon don't like each other like that anymore," Chloe defended Zee.

Zee looked at Chloe. Jasper was right—crashing into a guy was not the best way to flirt. But when it came to guys, Ally definitely knew her best. Even though Landon and Zee were just friends, Ally knew Zee still had a major crush on him!

As soon as she entered the cabin, Zee dropped her backpack onto the floor. The other girls rushed past her to claim their beds.

Ally climbed the ladder to the top bunk in the corner of the cabin. "Zee and I will sleep over here," she said.

Zee looked over at Chloe, who was standing by the bunks next to her.

"Yeah, that makes sense since Ally's your guest," Chloe

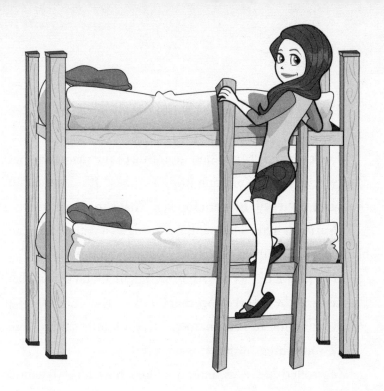

said. "You wanna share with me, Missy? You can take the top."

Missy tossed her sleeping bag on the bed above Chloe. "Okay. Thanks!"

Kathi and Jen claimed the last set of beds. "I'll be on top," Kathi declared.

Of course you will, Zee thought, since that's where perfect Kathi almost always landed anyway.

"This is so awesome!" Chloe said. "We're out in the middle of nowhere in a cabin with no electricity."

"Let me know when you get to the awesome part," Zee said.

"Look at this!" Missy said, pointing to the messages that covered the walls. "'Simone loves Thomas.' It's carved into the wood, so it will be here forever. That's so romantic."

"'Kari was here,'" Jen said, gesturing to a date written in black marker. "'Seven. Thirteen. Nineteen ninety-seven.'"

"'NT plus RB,'" Zee read, then sighed. "Don't you wish you knew if they stayed together?"

"Remind me to get a marker," Kathi loudly said to Jen. "I have something I want to write."

Zee rolled her eyes and wondered how long it would be before Kathi stopped dropping hints and told everyone about her new boyfriend. As Zee bent to get her backpack, something small and brown scurried past her. "Aaaaaaa!" she screamed, quickly climbing up the ladder to sit next to Ally. "I just saw a rat!"

Chloe moved toward the tiny creature, which was escaping through a small hole at the bottom of the wall. "It's not a rat. It's a mouse."

"Same thing," Zee said.

"Not hardly. Rats are bigger *and* lots smarter," Chloe explained. "That's why they make great pets."

"I think I'd rather have a dog," Zee said.

The other girls began to get set up.

"Where do you think the armoires are?" Kathi asked as she unpacked her brown leather Louis Vuitton bag. "I have to hang some of this stuff up before it wrinkles." Kathi hated any kind of imperfection. The phrase *roughing it* was definitely not in her vocabulary.

Missy's eyes grew big. She hadn't been at Brookdale Academy as long as the other girls, so some of Kathi's comments still shocked her. "You have to keep everything in your suitcase."

"Is housekeeping going to wash the dirty clothes?" Kathi asked.

"Um . . . there isn't any housekeeping," Missy said. "You have to take your dirty clothes home like that."

"You mean I have to mix my clean and dirty clothes in one bag?"

Missy nodded. "Mmm-hmm."

"I like Missy!" Ally whispered to Zee.

Zee smiled and whispered back, "She's cool."

"But I've got brand-new stuff in here!" Kathi continued.

"Some of it still has tags on."

"Why did you bring such nice stuff to camp anyway?" Chloe asked. "Didn't you get the information sheet and supply list?"

"I thought it was a joke," Kathi said, sounding defensive. "I mean, it listed 'sweatshirt.' Why would anyone wear something with the word *sweat* in the name?"

Zee hated to admit it, but she had to agree with Kathi on her fashion point. They were finally out of their horrible school uniforms. Why would they want to wear sweats?

"It doesn't matter," Kathi said, trying to change the subject. "I need to send a text message to *someone* before we go to the lodge anyway." She gave Jen a sneaky look.

"Who?" Zee asked, unable to stand Kathi's obvious hinting for one more minute.

"My boyfriend," Kathi said. "Trey Munson."

"You're going out with Trey Munson?" Ally asked. "He's soooooo hot!"

A proud smile spread across Kathi's face. "Yeah, he is."

"I thought Trey was going with Carrie Navatny," Chloe pointed out.

"That was last week," Jen put in. "Before Kathi told me to tell Trey she likes him."

As Kathi headed outside, the boys from cabin two

bounded into the girls' cabin. Conrad started snooping around their bags and bunks.

"So who's sleeping where?" Marcus asked.

"I'm over there with Missy," Chloe said, pointing to her bunk. "Zee and Ally are there. And Kathi and Jen are in the other one."

"Are you just keeping your bags under your beds or somewhere else?" Marcus continued.

"Zee's probably won't fit under the bed," Chloe said.

Marcus got excited. "Which one is hers?"

Zee looked over at Jasper and noticed he wore an uncomfortable expression.

"Well—" Chloe began.

"Wait!" Zee cut her off. She nodded to Jasper. "What's going on?"

Jasper straightened up his body—and his face. "Not a thing," he said.

"Still," Zee said. "I think I'll keep an eye on my bag." She dragged it closer to her. The boys were acting oddly. Was Zee going to have to watch out for them just as much as the bugs and bears?

3
Home Out of Range

The Beans followed the dirt path to the lodge. Kathi was already up ahead, and she was weaving to the left and right as she held her phone in front of her.

"What are you doing?" Jen asked when the group got closer.

"I can't get a signal!" Kathi sounded panicked.

"Maybe it's your service," Zee said. She pulled her iPhone out of her pocket. It had a bright blue skin with a big pink Z. "Nope, I don't have even *one* bar."

By now the students were wandering around in the forest, zigzagging past one another with their eyes fixed on their cell phones.

"Can anyone get any bars?" Missy asked.

"I can!" Conrad shouted. Everyone raced over to where he was now standing. "Oh, sorry," he said, wiping the screen on his shirttail. "That was just a bug."

"Ugh! This is like living in prehistoric times," Jen whined. "How did they survive?"

"We should tell Mr. P," Zee suggested. "He'll know what to do."

"He better," Kathi said as they moved along the trail. "My parents give a lot of money to the school. They won't be happy to hear I'm being treated this way."

"I don't think it has anything to do with money," Chloe said.

Kathi snorted. "*Everything* has to do with money."

The group hustled into the lodge. Students from other science classes were already seated and waiting for the orientation to begin.

Mr. P was at the front of the room. "You guys look like you've just run a mile," he told the Beans.

"We need your help," Zee told him.

"It's an emergency!" Kathi added.

Mr. P looked alarmed. "What is it?" he asked.

"We've been trying to use our cell phones, but we can't figure out where to go to get service," Zee explained.

"Oh, is that all?" Mr. P calmed down. "There's no service on Brookdale Mountain."

"Nowhere?" Conrad asked.

Mr. P shook his head. "No."

"As in . . . *no*where?" Marcus couldn't believe it, either.

Mr. P nodded.

"But what if there's an emergency?" Kathi said.

"Your parents have the camp phone number in their information packet," Mr. P explained. "And we can call from the office if we need to reach them. Plus, you can log on to the computers here in the lodge and use the internet to email them."

"Great!" Kathi said. "Where are they? I need to send an email now."

"*Now* we're going to have a meeting. During free time, everyone will have a chance. But since there are so many students and so few computers, there's a schedule." Mr. P held up a piece of paper.

The students leaned in to read the list. "Aaaaaa!" Kathi shrieked. "Cabin one isn't until the end of the week!"

"A whole week without our cell phones?" Zee asked.

"Or IMs?" Ally added.

"There's no one left to IM and email," Mr. P pointed out. "All your friends are here."

Kathi harrumphed. "My *boy*friend isn't here," she said. "What if he needs to talk to me?"

"Everyone should sit down now," Mr. P said, ignoring her. "The meeting's about to start."

The Beans sat together in the back of the room under an elk head that hung on the wall. "Gross!" Chloe groaned.

"At least he has a smile on his face," Conrad said. "Maybe he died happy."

"I bet he'd be happier running around in the woods," Chloe told him.

"Welcome to Brookdale Mountain, seventh graders!" Ms. Merriweather enthusiastically greeted the group. She'd pulled her blond hair into a ponytail under a baseball cap, and she wore a loose floral dress over a pair of black leggings. "I'm going to go over a few camp rules. First, no food in the cabins. Snacks will be available in the dining hall, and if anyone brought any food with them to camp, we can keep it in the kitchen."

Zee tried to listen, but her mind wandered, and soon she was planning a makeover for Ms. Merriweather.

A shorter skirt would look great on her, Zee thought.

"No leaving cabins after lights-out—unless it's for an outhouse emergency."

Her face would look brighter with lipstick.

"Everyone will have a work assignment each day."

Huh? Zee thought. This was beginning to sound like even more work than school.

"We'll post the lists on the cabin doors," Ms. Merriweather continued.

"These lists are killing me," Zee mumbled.

Ally turned to her. "Do you think I'll have to work since I'm not an actual student?"

"You should have to do even *more* work since you're not paying tuition," Jen said. Zee couldn't tell if she was kidding.

"Now, let's get to why we're here—the Science Scavenger Hunt," Ms. Merriweather said, holding up a disposable digital camera and sheet of paper over her head. "This is a list of plants and animals that are on Brookdale Mountain. The class that finds and photographs the most items on the list by Friday will win the scavenger hunt."

Jasper's serious face lit up. "Brilliant!" he cheered. Chloe gave him a thumbs-up.

Marcus raised his hand. "Are we going to have *any* fun?" he asked.

"Yes," Ms. Merriweather said, laughing. "We'll have lots

of outdoor activities and build campfires in the evenings. We'll even roast marshmallows some nights."

"And don't forget the talent show on Friday!" Mr. P called out from the side.

Yay! Zee silently applauded. She had a few ideas for what the Beans could perform together and couldn't wait to talk to the other band members about them. She was sure the Beans' performance would be the perfect way to end the week.

Hi, Diary,

Who cares about schoolwork, chores, and wooden toilets?* And so what if there's no communication with the outside world?! As long as I've got my best friends and the Beans, I've got all I need. Except my parents. ☹ But I haven't had a chance to miss them, and with everything I have to do, maybe I won't ever have a chance.

I'm totally tired already, though. My body feels like the camp bus ran over it. And the day is only halfway over!

Zee

* Okay, I've thought about it, and that one actually still bothers me a ~~little~~ lot.

4

Beans Breakdown

"*T*his is so cool!" Jasper said. He stopped beside the trail the fifth-period science students were walking on and bent down to get a better look at a bright orange plant. "I've never seen one of these before."

"That's because they only grow in California," Conrad told him.

"How do you know so much about plants?" Jasper asked.

"My grandmother likes me to help in her garden," Conrad explained.

"I thought you lived in an apartment," Zee said.

"Yeah. After Obachan moved in with me and Dad, she missed her garden so much, she volunteered to do the gardening for the whole building."

"Then you should be a big help to us. We have to find a million things for the scavenger hunt," Zee said, staring at a mysterious bug dodging the air in front of her. "And I'd like to do it as quickly as possible so we can get back to a bug-free zone."

Chloe lifted a rock.

"*What* are you doing?" Kathi asked.

"I'm looking for worms and bugs and lizards," Chloe told her.

Kathi looked like she was going to barf. "Why? They're gross."

Ally backed away from Chloe, and Zee giggled. She didn't plan to come in contact with creepy crawlies on purpose, either.

"They're all animals. They're really no different from dogs . . . or that chipmunk over there." She pointed into the woods. "Awwww! He's so cute."

Kathi huffed. "He is pretty cute, but my dog is a

purebred cockapoo. We paid three thousand dollars for him. Chipmunks cost nothing, which means they're worth nothing."

"My mom says the best things in life are free," Marcus put in.

"Your mother's wrong," Kathi said, curling her lip.

"Just trying to help," Marcus mumbled.

"If we don't start finding stuff soon, we're going to fail," Landon said, changing the subject.

"Landon's right!" Zee agreed, a little too enthusiastically. "I mean . . . um . . . that's what we're here for. Uh . . . not that you didn't know that." She could feel her face turning red. "I'll stop talking now."

Everyone held a copy of the scavenger hunt list. Next to each item's name was a photo of the plant or animal. Ally examined her sheet, then pointed to a picture of a tree with oblong leaves. "Let's look for this."

"Okay," Zee agreed.

Leaves crunched and rustled under her feet as Zee explored the woods with the Beans. But she could hardly concentrate on her assignment. Her mind kept wandering to the talent show. If they were going to be ready to perform on Friday, they needed to start planning right away.

"I was thinking the Beans should perform 'Forever Fabulous' for the talent show," Zee blurted out to the group.

"Is that the song you wrote?" Kathi asked.

Zee nodded. "Yeah."

"That would be adorable!" Kathi told her.

"Great!"

"But I can't."

"Why not?"

"I have a different idea," Kathi explained. "I want to do a duet with Missy—kind of a dueling violins routine."

A smile broke across Missy's face. "That sounds like so much fun."

"Doesn't it?" Kathi said through gritted teeth.

Ohmylanta! Zee thought. *Kathi doesn't care about having fun. She just wants to beat Missy.* And now thanks to Kathi, the Beans couldn't perform together. Zee was really disappointed.

Ally put her arm over her best friend's shoulder. "Cheer up!" she said, giving Zee a squeeze. "Now you don't have to worry about Kathi ruining the show for you," she whispered, then added, "Poor Missy. She doesn't know what she's in for."

Marcus, Conrad, Jasper, and Landon broke from the huddle they were in. "We're going to do a comedy sketch," Conrad announced.

"We need a girl to be in it," Marcus told the others.

Looking suspicious, Chloe shook her head. "Not me."

Landon eagerly looked at Zee.

"I'll do it!" Jen said.

Darn! Zee thought.

"If you take a girl, we should get a boy," Ally said.

"We're not trading cards," Conrad pointed out.

"Don't worry," Ally said. "We'll leave you with your friends." Her eyes locked on Jasper.

"I suppose I could do it," Jasper agreed.

"Good—because we're going to give you a makeover," Ally told him.

Jasper frowned. "What exactly do you mean?"

"Yeah, what are you gonna do?" Chloe sounded excited.

"You'll be the lead singer and Zee, Chloe, and I will be your band," Ally explained. "We'll make you really hot—like Justin Timberlake."

"Yes!" Zee cheered. "We can do choreography and sing."

"I don't think I know how to be *hot*," Jasper protested.

"Take off your glasses," Ally said.

Jasper did. "I can't *see*," he explained, squinting.

"You don't have to see," Ally told him. "You just have to sing—and look good."

"That's not going to be easy," Zee heard someone mumble behind her. She turned to see Landon standing nearby.

"What did you say?" Chloe asked him, placing a hand on her hip.

"Nothing," Landon said. Then he turned around and pretended to look for someone behind him.

Ohmylanta! Zee thought. She didn't know why Landon and Jasper had trouble getting along. But she liked both boys, and she didn't want to have to choose between them.

Chloe looked at Zee as Landon walked away. "Why would he say something like that?"

"I guess he just knows how uncomfortable Jasper is when he's not wearing his own style," Zee explained with a nervous giggle.

"Uh-huh," Chloe said, but she didn't look convinced.

Jasper put his glasses back on and looked at Landon. "On second thought," he began, "I'm looking forward to being *hot*."

That night all the seventh graders gathered around the campfire for a singalong.

"The other day," the boys belted out.

"The other day," the girls echoed, sitting on tree stumps.

"I met a bear," the boys came back.

"I met a bear," the girls repeated.

"Out in the woods."

"Out in the woods."

"A-way out there."

"A-way out there."

Then together the group sang, "The other day/I met a bear/out in the woods/a-way out there."

At first, Zee joined in on every round of call and response. Then she felt a tightness in her belly, and her face twisted in pain.

"What's wrong?" Ally asked.

"I don't know," Zee told her. "My stomach hurts."

Ally looked concerned. "What do you think it is?"

The pain went away as quickly as it had come. "I'm fine," Zee said. "It's nothing."

Zee started singing again. But she had to stop when another twist of pain made her double over. "Ohhhh," she groaned, clutching her stomach.

"Omigosh!" Chloe said. "Maybe you should go to the camp nurse."

"It's just a stomachache—probably from that delicious ground beef medley they called dinner," Zee said.

"But we all ate it," Jasper pointed out.

"Except me," said Chloe, who was a vegetarian and got the tofu medley instead.

"The point is," Jasper continued, "that no one else is sick."

"Do you feel like you're going to throw up?" Ally asked.

"No," Zee said. But what could make her stomach hurt this much all of a sudden?

Kathi leaned over. "Maybe you have a disease."

Ally swung her head so that her brown hair whipped around like a horse's tail. "She doesn't have a disease. It's just a little stomachache."

"Kathi's right," Jen said. "I saw a show on TV about a girl who was really, really sick and—"

"She's not 'really, really' sick!" Chloe said.

"Whatev," Kathi said dismissively.

"You're not really, really sick, are you?" Chloe whispered to Zee.

"Actually, I feel okay now," Zee told her friends. "It doesn't hurt anymore."

As the campfire died down, some of the seventh graders

in other classes went back to their cabins, but fifth period was having too much fun to go anywhere.

"Let's tell ghost stories," Conrad suggested.

"Okay," Ally said.

"Don't make them too scary," Chloe pleaded.

"Just keep reminding yourself there's no such thing as ghosts," Ally told her.

"Maybe not," Marcus said. "But there is such a thing as the Mountain Man."

"You know about the Mountain Man?" Zee asked. Maybe Adam wasn't lying after all.

Marcus nodded. "He tried to attack my older brother Jordan when he went on the science trip."

Ally shook her head. "Yeah, right."

"You don't believe in him?" Chloe asked her.

"No," Ally said. "Because he's not real. Right, Zee?"

"Well . . ." Zee hesitated, looking from Ally to Chloe to Marcus. "Maybe if he's just a really creepy guy who lives in the woods, he could exist. I mean, *people* are real."

"I *know* he's real," Marcus said.

"How?" Zee asked.

Marcus's eyes looked serious behind his dark-framed glasses. "Because of what happened to my brother."

"Really?"

Marcus nodded. "A fog had settled on the mountain," he began. "Jordan and his friends were on the trail, but the fog was so thick, they couldn't see three feet in front of themselves."

Zee leaned closer.

"Then, out of nowhere—" Marcus's voice suddenly got loud, startling Zee. "He reached out and grabbed Jordan. He screamed, but everybody else just ran. No one stayed to help him. Just as the Mountain Man started to drag Jordan deeper into the woods, the Mountain Man grunted, 'My leg! Something's got my leg.'"

"Give me a break," Ally said under her breath.

"What had his leg?" Chloe asked.

"Jordan never found out." Marcus breathed a sigh of relief. "He managed to pull free and ran away as fast as he could."

"That's ridiculous!" Ally said.

"Adam told us the Mountain Man said something about his leg," Zee reminded Ally.

"Since when do you believe Adam?"

Chloe wore a terrified expression. Zee was sure she believed the Mountain Man was real.

As Zee looked around to see if she could tell what the others were thinking, her eyes fell on Landon, who was looking right back at her. Somehow he made her even more nervous than the Mountain Man. Lately, he always seemed to be watching her.

Does Landon know I still have a crush on him? She would be humiliated if he did, since she was certain he liked her only as a friend.

Or maybe, Zee silently continued, *Landon actually does have a crush on me, too.* She shook the thought out of her head. It was too much to ask for. Zee nervously turned away from Landon.

Mountain Manhunt

Hi, Diary.

$\mathcal{Z}$ee stopped writing and thought. And thought. And thought. Nothing came. Even with everything that had happened that day, her mind was blank. Too exhausted to think anymore, she closed her diary. Whatever she had to say would just have to wait until she'd gotten a good night's sleep.

Walking to the cabin from the bathhouse, Zee dragged her feet. Her body was achy and tired. Even the toothpaste and brush felt heavy. She couldn't wait to collapse on her bunk and close her eyes.

"Hey, Zee!" Jen called behind her.

Ohmylanta! Zee thought. Talking to anyone—especially Jen—felt like torture at the moment. "What's up?" she asked.

Jen hurried to catch up with Zee. "I saw the way Landon was looking at you over the campfire." She made kissy noises.

"Really? What do you mean?" Zee asked.

"You two should totally go out!"

Zee shook her head. "We're just friends."

"I don't know," Jen said in a singsong voice. "I thought you had a big crush on him."

"Well," Zee responded. "Like I said, we're just friends."

"Mmm-hmm," Jen said skeptically.

"What aboout Kathi?" Zee asked. In sixth grade, Kathi and Landon had been boyfriend and girlfriend for a while.

"Pfffft," Jen muttered. "She so doesn't care anymore. Seventh-grade boys *do not* interest her." Then she walked off.

As Jen strode ahead, Zee couldn't stop thinking about what she had said. Maybe Jen was right. Maybe Landon did feel the same way about her that she felt for him.

But Zee had told her parents that she wasn't ready for a boyfriend. How could she go back on her word? Now she was *really* confused!

By the time Zee got back to the cabin, thoughts were bouncing all around her head. Thoughts about Landon. The other girls talked in the glow of their flashlights. Zee was glad to listen and be distracted from her thoughts.

"This cabin is so disgusting," Kathi whined.

"Oh, I wouldn't complain too much," Missy said. "When my mom was with Doctors Without Borders, we saw how people in other parts of the world really live. There are tons of people who would be happy to live in a place as nice as this."

Ally swung her head around to face Missy. "Your mom worked for Doctors Without Borders?"

"Do you know about them?" Missy asked.

"Yeah. In France we call it Médecins Sans Frontières," Ally told her. "My parents wrote a story about the organization."

"That's so awesome!" Missy said.

"What country were you in?" Ally asked.

"Uganda, Kenya, and Zambia. We moved around Africa," Missy explained.

Zee smiled. Ally fit right in with the new group. Even though it's not something that Ally and Zee had in common, the fact that Ally lived in a different country actually meant she had more in common with Jasper and Missy.

Zee was so happy to be with her friends. Maybe her worries about Landon weren't such a big deal after all.

Exhausted from the busy day, Zee floated off to sleep, but a pain in her side woke her up. When it happened again, she began to worry. As quietly as she could, Zee clicked on her flashlight, opened her diary, and continued with the entry she had started earlier.

I'm scared. My stomach hurts—and not like when I eat too much. This is totally different—like someone is squeezing my insides.

What if Kathi is right and I have a horrible disease? I read an article once in Flip magazine about a girl who got really, really sick because she didn't wash her hands. Then she got a bad infection and went into a coma. After the doctors saved her, she wrote a book *about it. Maybe I should have read the book. Then I wouldn't be sick right now.*

I think I'll go wash my hands.

Zee

Zee tiptoed across the cabin toward the door. As she reached for the handle, she heard grunting. *Ooog ooog.* Then a horrible scraping sound. *Screech screech screech.* The Mountain Man!

Zee was so afraid, she froze. Nothing moved, except for her trembling hand. Without thinking about it, she rushed over to Ally, reached up to the top bunk, and shook her best friend. "Ally!" she whispered. "Wake up!"

Ally's eyes barely opened. "What is it?" she grumbled.

"I think the Mountain Man is outside."

"We can check it out in the morning," Ally told her, rolling over in her sleeping bag. "I just want to sleep."

Zee looked around in the dark, then moved toward Chloe. "*Psst*. Chloe," Zee barked in a whisper.

Chloe's eye popped open. "What's going on?" she asked, worried.

"I think the Mountain Man is outside," Zee told her.

"Let's find out!" Chloe grabbed her flashlight. Zee followed as Chloe raced toward the door.

"Wait for me," Ally said, carefully climbing down the ladder in the dark.

"I thought you were too tired," Zee pointed out.

"I changed my mind. I don't believe in ghosts and monsters," Ally said, "but it might be fun to look."

6
Period?
Exclamation Point!

Snap. A twig broke under Zee's feet.

"*Shhh,*" Ally said, leaves crackling as she stepped.

"It's impossible to be quiet out here," Chloe whispered. "There's so much stuff on the ground."

"We just need to watch where we walk," Ally told the other girls.

"I can't see anything," Chloe said in her softest voice. "Can you?" Her flashlight's beam danced from tree to tree.

"I guess we should have brought more than one flashlight," Zee said.

Chloe's beam settled on a huge figure in the distance.

"Aaaaaaa!" Chloe screamed.

"*Shh!*" Ally put her finger to her lips.

"Did you see him?" Zee asked Chloe.

"*Him?*" Ally asked. "It was probably a tree or a boulder or something."

"That was the Mountain Man! Trees and boulders don't move," Chloe said.

"How do you know it moved?" Ally asked. "You had your flashlight on it for, like, a second."

"Yeah, 'cause he moved."

"Ooow!" Zee cried out as pain twisted her stomach.

"*Shh!*" Chloe said softly.

"Sorry," Zee apologized. "My stomach hurts."

It was too late. The male chaperones' cabin squeaked open.

Mr. P stepped outside. "It's midnight. What are you girls doing out here?" He didn't sound happy.

"Ummm . . ." Ally paused for a second. "Zee's stomach hurts. We were just helping her to the bathhouse."

"In case she throws up," Chloe added.

"Are you all right, Mackenzie?" Mr. P asked seriously.

"Yes, it's just a little stomachache," Zee assured him. She felt horrible but not because of her stomach. The girls had just lied to Zee's favorite teacher. But what could they do? Even though Zee didn't mind talking about the mysterious creature with her friends, she wasn't quite ready to tell her teacher. Not until she had more evidence that the Mountain Man existed.

Back in the cabin, the other girls went right back to sleep, but Zee tossed and turned. Between her stomachache, the Mountain Man, and telling Mr. P a half-truth, her mind wouldn't stop whirring. There was only one thing to do. She pulled out her diary.

Hi, Diary,

It's me again. This must be a record—three times in one night!

I thought I'd be okay with my friends here, but it's definitely weird being out in the middle of nowhere without my parents. Who will protect me from the Mountain Man?

Shuffle. Shuffle. Squeak. Footsteps passed by Zee's cabin and entered another one.

That's weird, Zee thought. *I wonder what took Mr. P so long to get back to his cabin?* She quickly wrote her name at the bottom of the entry, pulled the sleeping bag over her head, and tried not to think about what was lurking outside.

"I'm ready!" Chloe announced the next morning. "Everybody, hurry up, or we'll be late for kitchen duty. We have to set up the dining hall for breakfast."

"We get to eat before we start working as long as we are there on time," Missy said. She looked as bright and cheerful as Chloe.

Zee was still half asleep, and her blurry eyes had trouble focusing on the girls. "I don't think I got even an hour of sleep last night."

"Chloe told me about what you saw outside," Jen said as she twisted a red ponytail holder around her thick hair. "Do you really think it was the Mountain Man?"

Zee tied the shoelace of her red Converse high-top. "Who else could it have been?" she asked. Then she stood with the others.

"Uh, Zee," Ally said, pointing at Zee's feet. "I don't think you want to go out like that."

"Ohmylanta!" Zee groaned. On her right foot, she had put on her polka dot Converse. She quickly replaced the polka dot sneaker with the other red high-top. They went best with the pink top and red shorts she'd quickly grabbed from her suitcase when she woke up just a few minutes before.

"Let's go to the dining hall!" Chloe cheered. Everyone moved toward the door, except Kathi.

"Are you coming, Kathi?" Jen wondered.

"You guys go ahead, and I'll come later," Kathi told her.

A cramp in Zee's stomach reminded her that she had more to worry about than the Mountain Man. "Ow!" she complained, clutching her middle.

"Oh my gosh!" Chloe said. "Is it your stomach again?"

"Yes," Zee explained. "I'm afraid something might be wrong."

"It's probably nothing," Ally said. "Once you eat, you'll feel better."

Chloe looked from Ally to Zee. "I dunno. I think you should visit the nurse."

"Oh yeah," Ally quickly said, slipping her hand through

Zee's arm. "I'll go with you if you want."

Zee waved her hand in the air dismissively. She realized the nurse might send her home. She'd love to be back with her parents, sleeping under her cozy comforter at night and taking a warm shower in the morning, but she was not going to miss all the camp fun. "You guys go ahead. I'll meet you at the dining hall." She grabbed the mesh bag she'd decorated with Jibbitz. "I still have to go to the bathhouse."

"Okay," Chloe said, "but don't take too long. We don't have much time before the other seventh graders get there. You don't wanna miss breakfast."

"I'm not so sure about that," Ally said.

"What do you mean?" Chloe asked.

"Breakfast might be horrible," Ally told her. "It's not exactly French cuisine."

"Zee and I usually don't eat French food anyway," Chloe pointed out. "American food will be okay."

Zee started to worry what Chloe might think of Ally. Even though Zee knew Ally wasn't a snob, Chloe might get the wrong idea.

"You guys are never going to find out about the food unless you get there," Zee said, heading toward the bathhouse. "Save me a seat!"

In the bathhouse, Zee put her bag near the sink, then headed toward one of the stalls.

Zee unzipped her shorts and gasped. A spot dotted her underwear. She rubbed her eyes and looked again. Still there. Her heart pounded. She looked closer. Then her mind flashed back to a recent conversation with her mother. The phrases floated through her head. "Stomach cramps." "Tiredness." "Blood."

Suddenly, it all made sense. Zee had gotten her period!

"Ohmylanta!" Zee said. "Is that even possible?" The book called *Your Changing Body* that her parents had given her had said she'd get boobs first.

Wait! Zee thought. Maybe she'd missed something. Maybe she *had* gotten boobs in the middle of the night. Excited, Zee looked down, but she was disappointed. She was as chest-free as ever. *Figures.*

Zee had bigger problems, though. She didn't have any pads or tampons, and there wasn't a drugstore for miles. What would she do? Where would she get some? Normally, if she needed a teacher's help, she'd ask Mr. P, but it wasn't like *he'd* have any pads.

After quickly brushing her teeth, Zee headed back to the cabin. She needed to change her underwear and figure out how to get supplies.

Kathi was stretched out on her bunk, furiously typing on her BlackBerry.

"Are you still here?" Zee asked.

Kathi didn't look at Zee or stop typing. "Obviously."

"But you're supposed to be helping out with kitchen duty," Zee said. "Don't you want to have breakfast?"

"I'd rather miss breakfast than serve slop," Kathi said. She typed with one hand as she reached into a bag that was next to her and pulled out a breakfast bar. "Besides, I've got my own stash."

"We're not supposed to have food in the cabin," Zee reminded her.

Kathi shrugged. "Whatev," she said. "Let's see Brookdale Academy kick me out. They'd have to kiss my parents' big checks good-bye."

Zee knew the no-food-in-the-cabin rule was to keep animals out. The last thing she wanted was to bunk with a raccoon—all because of Kathi's selfishness. But Zee didn't feel like confronting Kathi at the moment, so she changed the subject. "So can we send text messages now?"

"No, I was just typing a few to send out when they rescue us."

"Rescue us? From what?"

"Look around," Kathi said. "This isn't exactly the Four Seasons. I was brought here under false pretenses."

"You were? What did they tell you it would be like?" Zee asked.

"Well, not like *this*. I had no idea *anyone* would volunteer to live like this." Kathi paused, then added, "No offense."

"For what?"

"It seems like this is your kind of thing," Kathi explained. "Don't you make your own clothes?"

"Sometimes. What's that got to do with it?"

"Nothing," Kathi said quickly. "Anyways, I'm sure my boyfriend is worried about me."

"Why?" Zee asked.

"I guess you wouldn't understand since you've never had one."

Zee stiffened. "I guess."

Kathi's eyes squinted at Zee. "Hey! Why aren't *you* on kitchen duty?"

Zee sighed. She really didn't want to tell Kathi her news, but she was desperate. Kathi was the only human being around at that moment. With her tall body and big boobs, Kathi looked more like a freshman in high school than a seventh grader. She probably knew more about periods than anyone else in the cabin.

"I just got my period," Zee blurted out.

In an instant Kathi had Zee in a hug. "That's so awesome. You're a woman!" Kathi said, then added, "Even though you don't look like one."

"There's just one little problem," Zee said, ignoring Kathi's remark. "I don't have anything with me—you know, like pads."

"No prob." Kathi hurried over to her shoulder bag and pulled out a package. "You can have these."

Zee looked at the pouch Kathi had handed her. "I can have all these? Don't you need them?"

"No. I brought them just in case. You're going to need to start doing that, too."

Zee took out a pad and slipped the rest in her tote bag. "Thanks for the tip."

"Oh, I can give you lots of advice," Kathi explained. "Now we can be in a secret club together."

"Secret?"

"You know, so people who don't understand don't try to get in."

Zee flashed on Ally and Jasper's conversation about London on the bus. And Ally and Missy's conversation about living abroad in the cabin. Zee felt a twinge of jealousy tighten inside her. It would be nice to have something special to share with someone—even if it was with Kathi.

"Cool beans," Zee said.

"GWP."

"GWP?"

"Girls with Periods," Kathi said matter-of-factly. "It's code, so no one knows what we're talking about."

"Oh, right." Zee was in shock—but not about getting her period. Was Kathi really asking her to be in the same club? "Are there any other members?" Zee asked.

"Jen hasn't gotten hers yet," Kathi said. "Have Chloe and Ally?"

Zee shook her head slightly. She felt weird about sharing such personal information about her best friends with Kathi.

"What about Missy?" Kathi asked.

"I don't know," Zee said.

Kathi thought a second, then mumbled, "Maybe I finally beat her in something."

Zee jumped when the cabin door opened with a *thud*. "Ms. Merriweather says you two need to come right now if you don't want to be on cleanup duty," Ally told them. "I had to beg her to let me leave to warn you."

"Okay," Zee said. "I just need a second to put my pad in." She flashed an excited grin and held up the square blue package.

Zee expected Ally to jump up and down or hug her like Kathi had or . . . something. Instead, Ally just calmly said, "Oh, you got your period?"

Zee's smile melted. Kathi leaned close to her ear. "See? You have to be in the club to understand," she whispered. Then she headed toward the door and in a normal voice said, "I'm out of here. The only thing grosser than serving institutional food to other people is cleaning up their disgusting leftovers."

As Zee watched Kathi move down the wooden steps, she felt a tug. Did she really feel closer to Kathi at that moment than to Ally?

* * *

Hi, Diary,

I have sooooo much to tell you! I didn't think I'd get my period until after everyone else. Like way after. But now I'm one of the first ones. I feel different and not-so-different all at once. It's like when you have your birthday, and mostly you're the same as the day before—but you're also a year older.

Unfortunately, I may not be the only one who has changed. Ally is acting funny. But not the good kind of funny. Why isn't my BFF happier for me? Don't best friends get excited about stuff like periods? I know I'd be sooo excited for her. Did I do something wrong?

Zee

7

Man Handled

"Hey, Jasper!" Chloe shouted. "Bring the camera over here. I think I found something." After breakfast, all the seventh graders were back in the woods looking for plants and animals for the scavenger hunt.

"Looks good to me," Ally said, making a check mark on their sheet.

"At this rate, I think we might actually win," Zee said excitedly, slapping the spot on her leg where a bug had just landed. "Too bad we don't have to find bugs. They keep coming to *me*."

"Maybe it's not such a good idea to wear shorts in the woods," Chloe said. She had on stretchy blue sport pants with a stripe down each side and a white long-sleeve T-shirt.

"But aren't they cute? Look at all the pockets," Zee said. "I got them just for camping."

"Then perhaps you should have applied some insect repellent," Jasper suggested.

"My mother provided me with numerous bottles of that, too."

"That's *such* a great idea, Jasper," Ally said.

Jasper blushed and looked at the ground. "Thanks."

Zee couldn't believe that Ally had actually found a way to flirt with Jasper over bug spray.

"What are they doing?" Chloe asked, pointing to Kathi and Jen, who were sitting on a huge boulder, reading magazines.

The fifth-period science class had divided up so they could find items faster. Zee, Jasper, Chloe, and Ally had ended up looking together in one part of the woods. Missy, Landon, Conrad, and Marcus were farther down the path.

"What they always do," Ally said. "Avoiding work."

"I thought Kathi got straight As," Jasper put in. "How can that be?"

"She makes sure the group she's in works hard to get an A for her," Ally explained.

"Maybe Kathi is the Mountain Man," Chloe suggested. "You know—to scare us all so much, we have to end the field trip and go back home."

"I don't think so," Zee said. "She was in the cabin last night."

"Oh yeah," Chloe said, looking disappointed.

"Still, I'd be happy if I never heard creepy groaning noises like that ever again," Zee said.

"That was probably just my stomach growling. I was pretty hungry when I went to bed," Ally joked.

"Well, unless your stomach can throw its voice outside the cabin, I don't think so," Zee said. "And it certainly wasn't you limping into the woods."

"We're not sure we saw anything limping in the woods," Ally said.

"Did you guys hear anything in your cabin, Jasper?" Chloe asked. He had moved a few feet down the trail and was searching around for other scavenger hunt items.

"I was exceedingly tired last night," Jasper said without looking up at the girls.

"What if there really is a Mountain Man?" Zee wondered out loud.

"There's not," Ally insisted.

"How do you know?" Chloe said.

"Who was the first person to ever mention the Mountain Man?" Ally asked.

Zee thought. "I guess it was Adam."

"Exactly." Ally nodded.

"Why wouldn't Adam tell the truth?" Chloe asked.

"Because he loves to make Zee crazy. And it's working."

Out of nowhere, a loud cry echoed through the woods.

"That sounds like Conrad!" Chloe said.

Zee, Chloe, Ally, and Jasper rushed down the dirt path toward the noise. Even Kathi and Jen got off their rock to see what was happening. When they reached the other group, Conrad was lying on the ground. Marcus and Landon were huddled around him. Missy ran over from where she had been hunting for specimens.

"What happened?" Missy called out.

"Something grabbed me from behind and started dragging me away," Conrad explained. His voice was shaking and scared. "When I screamed, he let go."

Tingles ran up Zee's spine as she noticed the tracks from

Conrad's body being dragged.

"The Mountain Man," Zee whispered.

"What did you say?" Marcus asked.

"I think it might have been the Mountain Man," Zee said. "Did you see anything, Missy?"

Missy shook her head. A couple of tiny leaves stuck out of her silky brown hair, and a trail of dirt streaked her forehead. "No. Conrad thought it would be a good idea for me to go into the woods over there and look for stuff."

Conrad stood up. "I heard a ripping sound."

Zee gasped. "Look!" she said. A piece of flannel hung from the tip of a low tree branch. "That looks like part of a man's shirt. That must have been what you heard."

Kathi twisted up her face. "Ugh! If *that's* what he's wearing, I hope he stays on the mountain."

Craaaaaack! The sound echoed loudly, cutting through the forest.

Zee grabbed Jasper's arm. "What was that?" she asked.

Marcus, Conrad, and Landon looked around. Conrad seemed even more terrified than he had before.

"Yeah, what was that?" Landon asked.

Ally eyed him suspiciously. "Have you guys found anything for the scavenger hunt yet?"

"Well . . . um . . . uh," Conrad stammered.

"I found a few things," Missy said, holding up the camera.

"Missy's the only one, huh?" Ally said.

"We do still have tons of items on our list," Marcus said.

Landon's face suddenly brightened like a lightbulb had gone off in his head. "I have an idea. Maybe Zee could work with us, too."

"Why?" Jasper quickly asked.

"Well, that way the groups would be more even, and Missy won't be the only girl," Landon explained.

"I don't think we should be penalized because you guys haven't found much," Jasper countered.

"It's not a punishment," Landon said. "We're all on the same team—fifth-period science."

Jasper turned to Zee. "Don't you want to be with your friends?"

Flustered, Zee almost couldn't speak. She felt caught in the middle of her best friend and the boy she had a huge crush on.

"Umm . . . yeah . . . ," Zee said. "But everyone here is my friend." She looked at Landon and Jasper. And Chloe and Ally. "Everyone is friends with everyone. Right?"

The Beans stared at one another awkwardly. Missy, Conrad, and Marcus looked confused. Kathi and Jen looked smug. Landon and Jasper looked angry. And Chloe looked like she was biting her tongue.

Ally took Jasper's arm and guided him away from the group. "Come on! Let's get back to work."

"You're awfully serious about the scavenger hunt," Kathi said to Ally.

"Even though you're not getting graded," Jen added.

Zee looked at Kathi and Jen. *Someone has to be,* she thought.

Ally put her arm around Zee. "I'm just looking out for my best friend."

Ohmylanta. Zee felt like a total idiot. Just because Ally didn't go nuts about Zee's period didn't mean they weren't still best friends forever. *Duh!*

"What happened after that?" Ally asked Missy. The two girls were talking about their travels as cabin one walked into the main lodge for afternoon cleanup duty.

"The plane made an emergency landing—right in the center of a big field!" Missy told her. "The villagers rushed over to say hello."

"Were they mad?"

"At first, they didn't know how to react," Missy began. "But my dad took out his digital video camera and started filming them." Missy's father was a documentary film-maker. "They loved seeing themselves."

"That's so cool!"

"And it turns out a woman was giving birth," Missy went on, "so my mother helped deliver the baby."

"Your parents have the most interesting jobs," Ally said. Zee felt a twinge of jealousy. Mr. Carmichael was the editor of *Gala* magazine and got to meet lots of celebrities. Until now Ally had always said he had the most interesting job.

Zee opened the lodge's utility closet. "Ms. Merriweather told us we should sweep up the floor and wipe off all of the surfaces," she reminded the girls. "We can divide up the work."

"I'll sweep," Chloe volunteered.

"Umm . . . okay," Zee said. "But there are just two brooms." Would she sweep with Chloe or dust with Ally?

Ally answered her question. "Missy and I can wipe everything off," she said, stepping into the closet to grab a pile of rags. She handed one to Missy, then held one out for Kathi.

"No thanks," Kathi said. "I'm not going to need that."

"Did you want to sweep instead of dust?" Zee asked.

Kathi and Jen rolled their eyes and giggled. "None of the above. We brought our magazines."

"But Ms. Merriweather said we could have free time if we finish quickly," Chloe reminded them.

"Then you better hurry," Kathi told her as she and Jen headed to a table in the middle of the room.

Chloe and Zee began sweeping the floor near the utility closet as Ally and Missy wiped off the large wooden chairs in the front of the room.

"I talked to the girls in cabin four, and second-period science has only about half of the stuff for the scavenger hunt," Chloe told Zee.

"We've got to beat them," Zee said. "I don't want the Mountain Man to keep us from winning."

"I hope Conrad isn't too scared to go back in the woods to look for stuff," Chloe said.

"We need all the help we can get," Zee agreed.

Chloe motioned toward Kathi and Jen. "I don't know who is scarier—the Mountain Man or them."

Zee swept a pile of dirt and small bits of paper into the dustpan. "Guess what?" she excitedly whispered to Chloe.

"What?"

"I got my period!"

"Get out of here!" Chloe said.

Zee nodded.

"When?"

"This morning," Zee said. "I've been dying to tell you, but there's always someone around."

"What's it like?" Chloe asked in a low voice.

"Actually, it doesn't really feel that different," Zee said. "I don't really notice it—except the pad is kind of weird."

"That must be why your stomach hurt," Chloe said. "You had cramps."

"I think so," Zee told her, "but they're gone now."

Chloe studied Zee. "This is so awesome!" She jumped up and down and squealed.

Ally looked up from her dusting. "Watch out!" she called. "You're going to spill all the dirt, and it'll take us longer to clean up."

"Oh, gosh! You're right," Chloe said. "I guess I got carried away by Zee's big news. I'm sure she told you right away."

"What big news?" Ally asked.

"About Zee's period," Chloe explained.

"Oh yeah, she told me this morning. I'm so psyched." Ally gave Zee a hug.

* * *

Hi, Diary,

You can never have too many best friends. Like Chloe and Ally! And Jasper. I feel kind of weird telling Jasper about my period. That's the problem with having a boy for a best friend. I guess since I can tell him everything else, it's no big deal.

Except I can't tell him about Landon, either. Not that there's anything to tell. Is there?

The coolest part is that Ally is friends with Chloe and Jasper, too. We're just one big happy group!

Zee

8

Practice Makes Problems

$\mathcal{L}$ater that day, fifth-period science gathered on the camp's wooden outdoor stage to practice for the talent show. After the lodge cleanup, Zee had changed into a skirt with leggings underneath and a long-sleeve gray T-shirt. She had gotten enough bug bites to understand that even when she wasn't scavenging deep in the woods, she needed to cover her arms and legs.

Zee, Chloe, Ally, and Jasper were all sitting cross-legged on the platform around Mr. P. "Have you guys decided on a song?" he asked.

"I was hoping we could sing 'Forever Fabulous'—since everyone knows it from music class," Zee said. "I have my guitar, Jasper has his bass, and Ally brought her flute, so she can play with us."

"And since I didn't bring my ginormous cello, I'll sing, too," Chloe said.

"Jasper is going to be the lead singer, though," Ally said.

"Sounds like you guys have it figured out," Mr. P said. "Now I think I need to go help Kathi and Missy."

Zee glanced over to the corner where the girls were practicing their violin duet. Kathi breathed fast, as if she might hyperventilate, while she watched Missy. Missy's bow smoothly danced across the strings, and her left hand quickly glided up and down her violin's neck. But if Missy noticed Kathi's panic, she didn't show it and stayed focused on getting the notes right.

When Mr. P walked away, Ally put her hand on Jasper's shoulder. "You are going to look so good," she told him. "We can do something really cool with your hair. Don't you think he's going to look hot, Zee?"

Zee could feel her face warm and wondered if it was as red as Jasper's. She could understand why Jasper was embarrassed, but why was she? Was it because of the way Ally was acting—or something else?

"Too bad your *boyfriend*, Jacques, can't come to see you perform, Ally," Zee said, sliding between her friends.

Ally stood to stretch her legs. "Oh, I don't think Jacques would be very interested in a school talent show." Then she sat down again—next to Jasper.

"Really? Has your *boyfriend* ever heard you perform before?" Zee asked.

Ally giggled and wrinkled her nose. "Zee, you're so funny. You keep saying 'boyfriend' like it's a bad word."

"Oh, I don't think it's bad at all," Zee defended herself. "I think it's great you have a boyfriend. Back in France. Named Jacques."

"Me too," Ally agreed.

"Ahem." Landon seemed to appear out of nowhere and was standing at the stage.

Without even thinking, Zee slid away from Jasper. "What's up?"

"Our group was wondering if you have a pipe cleaner, a Hula-hoop, and a skateboard," Landon said.

"For what?" Jasper asked.

"For our comedy sketch," Landon answered Jasper, even though he looked straight at Zee. She started to get an uncomfortable feeling and looked away.

"Are those things supposed to be humorous?" Jasper asked.

Landon finally turned his eyes away from Zee to Jasper,

giving him an exasperated look. "Dude, the *things* aren't funny, but what we do with them will be."

This time Zee put herself between the two boys. "I don't have any of that stuff. Sorry."

"Yeah, I didn't bring anything like that for the camping trip," Chloe said.

"Neither did I," Jasper said. "I neglected to pack my Hula-hoop."

Ally laughed harder than Zee had ever heard her laugh the entire time they'd known each other.

"Thanks anyway," Landon said, and smiled at Zee. "Later." He walked back to his group.

Zee watched Landon leave, then sat down. She could barely concentrate on the talent show. Why didn't Landon and Jasper get along? And why were Jasper and Ally getting along too well? Was everyone going crazy?

"How many of these do we have to put together anyway?" Kathi asked.

"Ms. Merriweather said we could stop after we've done one hundred," Zee said.

Kathi and Zee were making s'mores packets with Landon and Jasper for the campfire later. They sat around a square table, working together. Zee grabbed two graham crackers,

Jasper dropped in the chocolate, Landon added a couple of marshmallows, and Kathi sealed them in a bag.

"It feels like we've already done a hundred," Kathi said.

"Actually, we've done ten," Zee pointed out.

Landon popped a piece of chocolate into his mouth. "It could be worse," he said. "We could have to clean the bathrooms."

"That's not even funny," Kathi said. "I would be so out of here if I had to clean bathrooms."

"At least it's for a good cause," Zee said. "The campfire's going to be great."

"I've never been to a marshmallow roast before," Jasper said as he took a bite of graham cracker.

"Never?" Zee said. Jasper shook his head. "Cool beans!

It's so much fun—especially when you roast the perfect marshmallow. It's brown and gooey but not burnt. But mostly it's just fun hanging out with friends."

"Speaking of which," Kathi began, "it must be so fantastic to have Ally back in Brookdale."

"Definitely," Zee said. "Sometimes it feels like she never left."

Then Kathi turned to Jasper. "But I'm sure it's weird for you," she said to him.

"Wumpt?" Jasper asked. He'd just put another graham cracker in his mouth.

"You know, Zee's best friend having a crush on you," Kathi said.

A spray of graham cracker crumbs flew across the table. "Gross!" Kathi screamed, jumping up and frantically wiping her shirt.

Landon started laughing. "Go for it!" he said to Jasper. "Ally's cute."

Jasper's face turned as red as Zee's bob. Zee wasn't sure it would ever return to its normal pale shade.

After sputtering a few noises, Jasper managed to say, "Maybe *you* should 'go for it' if you think she's so cute."

"I don't think Ally is Landon's type at all," Kathi put in.

"Ally has a boyfriend," Zee said.

"Yes, that's right," Jasper said. "Jacques. From France."

"That doesn't mean she can't like Jasper, too," Landon explained.

"Actually, it does," Zee said. "Well, I think it does."

"I agree with Zee," Jasper quickly added. "I certainly wouldn't want my girlfriend to have a crush on someone else."

"Well, I wouldn't, either," Landon defended himself. "I just thought—"

"I'm done!" Kathi suddenly interrupted.

"But we still have a ton of packages to put together," Zee pointed out.

"Sorry, but I'm just not feeling well," Kathi said. She swooned a little so her hair swung back and forth across her shoulders. "All of this work is making me sick."

"It's okay," Landon said. "I can seal the bag after I put the marshmallows in."

"See ya!" Kathi waved as she walked away.

Now Zee was left with Landon and Jasper. *Awkward!* Zee thought.

Landon and Jasper did their jobs without looking up. Zee desperately wanted to fill the silence with words. But she couldn't think of a single thing to say. Instead she sat quietly, hoping a bear would come swallow her whole.

Later, as Zee approached cabin one, she heard murmuring. "You have a boyfriend?" Kathi said.

"His name is Jacques," Ally told Kathi.

"Isn't having a boyfriend so cool?" Kathi asked. "The presents. And flowers."

"Well, Jacques doesn't really buy me a lot of stuff, but we do talk and text all the time."

"That's almost as much fun!" Kathi said. "Is he older?"

"No, he's twelve, too—or should I say, '*douze.*'" Both girls giggled.

Zee opened the cabin door. "What were you guys talking about?" she asked.

Ally and Kathi looked at each other. Ally was about to say something, but at that moment, Jen, Missy, and Chloe arrived.

"Man, I'm tired," Chloe said, landing on her bunk.

"Well, at least we'll never have to collect firewood again," Missy said.

"Thank goodness!" Jen added. "That job is *the worst.*"

Ally closed her mouth as the other girls went on. Zee couldn't believe that Ally was confiding in Kathi. Ally always said she didn't trust Kathi. Had Kathi invited Zee's BFF to be in a secret club, too? This time a club that Zee couldn't join?

The Boyfriend Club? The Boobs Club? Zee wondered. *Why would Ally talk about her boyfriend to Kathi instead of me?*

Hi, Diary,

What's up with Ally and Kathi? Ally is always telling me not to trust Kathi, but they were laughing like they were BFFs.

And why can't Landon and Jasper get along?

Still, that's not my biggest Jasper problem. What if Jasper ends up liking Ally back? She already has a boyfriend. Would she choose Jasper or Jacques? What if Ally breaks Jasper's ♥? Will he want to be my friend anymore if I'm friends with her?

I'm so confused. Here's what my head looks like:

Me

Jasper ♥ Ally

Zee

9

Offbeat

At the campfire that evening, Zee listened to the activity around her.

"Cabin six is the best! We have more spirit than all the rest!" a group of girls cheered.

"No, you're not!" another group responded. "Cabin eight is totally hot!"

The two groups cheerfully shouted back and forth. One of the boys' cabins threw a Frisbee around while another played a loud game of cards.

The Beans were lined up on the log benches around the fire. Ally was between Zee and Missy, but she talked more to Missy than to Zee. So Zee talked to Chloe and Jasper. Jasper seemed happy to avoid Landon, who was in a quiet huddle with Conrad and Marcus.

Ohmylanta! Zee said to herself. The Beans were supposed to be working together. The camp trip had united other science classes, but it had broken up theirs.

"All right, dudes!" Conrad suddenly shouted to the other Beans. "Marcus and I have a story for you."

Cool beans! Zee said to herself. Maybe there was nothing to worry about after all.

"It's a true story," Marcus put in.

"Yeah?" Kathi asked. "How do you know?"

"It happened to a friend of a friend. His name was Michael." Everyone quieted down to listen and then Marcus went on. "One day Michael was at the mall with his mom. They had been shopping for about five hours and were really, really tired. So they went back to their car and discovered an old lady sitting in the front seat."

Chloe leaned forward. "How did she get in there?" she asked.

"They left the door unlocked," Marcus said. "'I was so tired,' the lady told them. 'I couldn't find my car, and I needed a place to rest.' Michael's mom offered the woman a ride home. 'That would be so nice of you,' the woman said. But when Michael and his mom got in the car, the old woman pulled off her wig!" Marcus's voice got more excited.

"Why?" Chloe asked.

"Because it wasn't an old lady at all—it was a man pretending to be a woman. And he was sitting on a hatchet!"

"Aaaaaa!" Jen and Chloe screamed.

"Oh, please," Ally said. "I've heard that one before."

"Really?" Chloe asked. "Do you know Marcus's friend's friend?"

"No, but it didn't really happen to his friend's friend—or anybody—because it's not true."

"Why would Marcus lie?" Chloe defended him.

"It's not lying," Ally said. "It's—"

"Okay, gang!" Mr. P shouted above the noise. "The other teachers and I are going to divide you up into groups for a drum circle."

"Awesome!" Landon, who was the Beans's drummer, said. "For once, the drums get to be the star."

"Everyone will get a percussion instrument and the group will play together," Mr. P continued.

"Who's the leader?" Kathi asked.

"There's no leader," Mr. P explained. "It's about creating

a sound together—not following someone else's sound."

"That seems kind of stupid," Kathi complained as Mr. P handed out small drums, castanets, and rhythm sticks. "I think I did this in preschool music class."

"Totally babyish," Jen agreed.

"But that's what the Beans are all about," Zee reminded them. "Creating a sound together."

"I thought it was about being stars," Kathi said.

Conrad adjusted an imaginary collar on his navy-blue T-shirt. "I thought it was about getting girls' attention," he said. He high-fived Marcus and Landon.

Landon looked over at Zee and Zee tried not to let the panicked feeling in her stomach creep up to her face. She still had no idea what to do when he looked her way.

"I guess the Beans are about those things—sort of," Landon said. "But tonight we're not the Beans. We're a drum circle. You know, we're still us, but we have a different purpose."

"And that is . . . ?" Kathi said.

"We're not going to play songs like we usually do," Landon said. "Instead we'll come together by creating a group rhythm."

Relief washed over Zee. She was glad someone else understood that the group had to bond together.

But two minutes after the group started clicking, clacking, and banging out rhythms, Zee started to worry again.

Missy and Ally kept whispering to each other. Marcus and Conrad were acting goofy, trying to crack Landon up. Jasper shot Landon dirty looks as if he was the problem. Of course, Kathi and Jen were acting too cool to participate.

Only Chloe was making an effort. She clicked along with her castanets, coaxing Zee with nods. Zee tried to get in sync, but her mind kept returning to the fact that the Beans were falling apart. And she had no idea how to fix them.

Hi, Diary,
What happened to the band? No one else seems interested anymore. Not even Ally. I mean, she seemed so happy when Mr. P made her part of the Beans, but during the drum circle, she acted like she didn't care.

Zee stopped writing and thought. That was it! The trouble with the Beans started after Ally arrived. The Beans had had problems before, but nothing like this.

Is Ally breaking up the Beans?

Zee

Mr. P banged on the cabin door. "Five minutes until lights-out, girls!" he yelled.

"Anybody need to go to the bathhouse?" Zee asked.

Chloe looked over the top of the book she was reading. "Nope," she said. "I want to finish this chapter tonight."

"I'm good," Ally told Zee. And a chorus of *no*s from the other girls followed.

"Okay," Zee said. "See you in five."

When Zee went outside, she heard a strange grumbling voice with a weird accent. "My leg."

Zee trembled and looked around. "Who's there?"

"Give me my leg," the voice demanded. It sounded as though it was getting closer.

The Mountain Man!

Zee rushed back into the cabin. "Did you hear that?"

she asked when she got inside.

Chloe had already put her book down. "I did!" she said.

"Me too," Missy said. With a suspicious expression, she added, "Are you sure it wasn't you?"

"No way!" Ally said. "Zee wouldn't do that to her friends. Plus, look how scared she is."

"I thought you didn't believe in the Mountain Man," Zee told her.

"I don't, but I believe you," Ally said. "If you say you heard something, then someone is definitely out there."

"Everyone grab a flashlight," Chloe commanded. "We're going to find the Mountain Man."

Kathi stood up.

"Are we going, too?" Jen asked her.

"I'm losing too much beauty sleep over this horrible creature," Kathi explained. "Not that I actually need it. The sooner we find out what's making all that noise, the better."

"What about lights-out?" Missy asked.

"We'll just have to take a chance that we'll get into trouble," Ally said. "This is really important."

The group stormed out of the cabin, shining their flashlight beams into the woods. But all they saw were trees. Silent trees.

Zee heard voices coming from the boys' cabin. She pointed her flashlight at it. "If we heard something, maybe they did, too."

As the girls approached the cabin, Zee could hear what the boys were saying.

"Who's your favorite band, Jasper?" Marcus asked.

"I suppose that would be GMT," Jasper said. "They're a British band."

"Greenwich Meantime?" Landon asked.

"Do you know them?" Jasper said. The moody tone he had been using with Landon earlier had disappeared.

"Yeah," Landon told him. "I just downloaded their new CD."

Ally stormed into cabin two. "All right! Which one of you lost a leg?" she demanded. The other girls followed.

"Huh?" Landon said.

"Did you find an extra one?" Jasper asked, cracking Marcus and Conrad up.

"Didn't you guys hear a voice outside?" Chloe asked.

A puzzled look spread across Conrad's face. "No."

"Maybe because we were talking," Marcus said.

"We heard the Mountain Man!" Chloe announced.

"He said something to Zee!" Ally added.

In an instant, the room buzzed with excitement, and everyone started talking about this latest evidence. Zee looked from one seventh grader to the next and smiled to herself. If the Mountain Man could get the Beans back together like this, maybe he wasn't so bad after all. Still, she didn't plan on going to the bathhouse by herself anymore.

10

Fiddling Around

The next morning, the girls finally had to take their turn at the worst camp job assignment—breakfast cleanup, which meant helping the camp staff get the dishes ready to be washed after breakfast. Which meant dealing with half-eaten slop.

Knowing cabin one had to clean up the mess, cabin two's trays were especially disgusting. Marcus mixed his eggs with his milk. Conrad made a revolting statue out of his sausage and fruit. "Ew!" Missy said when she saw it. "That looks like a pile of vomit."

Just then one of the camp staff members came out of the kitchen with a bucket of fruit and vegetable scraps. "Does anyone want to take this out to the

compost bin?" she asked.

"I do!" Missy's hand shot up.

"I do!" Zee, Ally, Chloe, and Jen echoed.

The staff member handed the bucket to Missy. "Sorry, guys," Missy said. "I called it."

"Darn it!" Zee said. "I had no idea you cared so much about composting."

"Until this moment, neither did I."

As Missy left with the bucket, the other girls began cleaning up the tables.

"Ewww!" Jen screamed. She hadn't noticed that Landon had wrapped chewed-up food in a napkin—until she picked it up.

"It's a good thing Jasper never leaves food behind," Chloe joked as she placed his empty plate on the top of the growing stack.

"Where's Kathi?" Ally asked.

"I bet she's giving herself a manicure and pedicure back

at the cabin," Chloe said.

"Or she hired someone to come give her one," Ally added, laughing.

Zee slid a lump of unidentifiable food into the trash can. "I wish Kathi had hired someone to do her camp chores," she said. "I don't think she's done one thing since we got here."

"Do you know where she is, Jen?" Chloe asked.

"Remember?" Jen began. "She said she had to go to the bathhouse."

"Wasn't that a while ago?" Chloe pressed her.

"I guess," Jen said. Then she walked away from the group.

"Maybe she has her period, too," Ally suggested.

"I don't think so," Zee said. "She gave me her supply of pads." That's when she remembered. "Oh no!"

"What?" Ally asked.

Zee leaned close and whispered, "I forgot to bring a pad."

Chloe looked worried. "Are you . . . okay?"

"For now," Zee said. "But I'm a little nervous without an extra."

"You should go get one," Chloe suggested. "You don't want to have a . . . problem."

"Chloe's right," Ally agreed. "We can do your work until you get back."

"You guys are the best," Zee told her friends. She quickly headed to the cabin. From a distance, she could hear violin music. *That's weird*, Zee thought. The closer she got to the cabin, the louder the sound got. When she opened the door, she saw Kathi playing frantically.

The door shut, and Kathi stopped abruptly. Then she slid her violin behind her back. "What are you doing here?"

"What are *you* doing?" Zee shot back. "You're supposed to be working."

Kathi let the violin drop to her side and sighed. "This is the only time I can practice for the talent show." She sounded desperate.

"But we'll all get to practice our acts after lunch," Zee pointed out.

"I need to do it in private—without Missy."

"She's performing with you. Why would you want to practice without her?"

"Because it was *my* idea and *my* song, and she's still beating me."

Zee shook her head, confused. "But there

isn't any winning or losing. It's just for fun."

"Wake up, Zee." Now Kathi sounded impatient. "Everything is a competition. Just ask Ally."

"What does Ally have to do with this?"

"Isn't it obvious?" Kathi asked. "She can't stand to see you doing better than her."

"But I'm not doing better—or worse."

"That's not what she thinks," Kathi told her. "She hates the fact that you got your period."

"How do you know?" Zee asked suspiciously. Had Ally confided in Kathi about how she felt?

Kathi ignored Zee's question. "And she obviously can't stand that Jasper has a crush on you."

"Wha—but—" Zee could barely get her words out. "Jasper and I are just f-f-friends!" she protested.

Kathi put her violin back under her chin. "Whatev."

Zee was so flustered she hurried out of the cabin toward the dining hall. It was true that Ally had been acting a little weird on the trip, but what Kathi had said just couldn't be true. No matter what, Ally and Zee were BFFs. *Right?*

"Ohmylanta!" Zee mumbled and stopped abruptly. She'd forgotten what she'd gone to the cabin for in the first place. She spun around. And came face-to-face with Landon.

"Aaaaa!" Zee screamed, startled.

"Is everything all right?" Landon asked. Under the gaze of his warm blue eyes Zee felt like she was melting.

"Oh . . . uh . . . yeah . . . sure," Zee said. "I just went to the cabin and was totally surprised. And it's strange hanging out with Ally again. I mean, it's great and all, but Jasper—" She stopped when she realized she was rambling.

"What about Jasper?" Landon asked.

Zee shook her head. "Nothing." She really didn't know what was confusing her about her friend. And she knew that even if she *could* explain it to Landon, she wasn't sure she should. Normally, Zee would be thrilled to run into Landon on his own, but now she

just needed to get away to sort out her thoughts.

Up ahead on the path, Zee saw the perfect distraction. Missy and Jen were heading toward them going to cabin one.

Zee's relief lasted about a second. *Oh no!* she thought. She didn't want Missy to catch Kathi practicing by herself. There was something really sad about the fact that Kathi was so desperate. Zee would hate for anyone else—especially Jen, who for some weird reason admired Kathi—to see her like that.

"Uh . . . I gotta go," Zee told Landon.

"Oh . . . um . . . okay," Landon said.

"Hi, Missy," Zee called out as loudly as she could and rushed toward the girls.

"Are you okay, Zee?" Jen asked.

"Yes," Zee shouted, spinning around to face the cabin. "I am, *Jen*. How are you—AND MISSY?"

All of a sudden, Kathi zipped out of the

cabin and stood next to the group. She gave Zee the slightest "thank-you" nod.

"What's up, guys?" Kathi asked.

"Ms. Merr—" Missy began, but Jen cut her off.

"You're acting kind of weird, Zee," Jen pointed out.

"N-n-n-no I'm not," Zee protested.

"We just saw you talking to Landon alone. Does it have something to do with him? Are you guys going out now?" Jen persisted.

Zee gulped, hoping to use the extra time to get a response together. *Just say no*, Zee told herself. *That's the truth.* "Wh . . . uh . . . huh?"

Kathi stepped closer. "No way!" she said. "Zee needs someone as mature as she is—you know, because she's a woman now."

"She is?" Jen said. "She's twelve."

"You don't understand," Kathi said, putting her arm around Zee's shoulder.

Zee's body stiffened. She hated to have Kathi speak for her. But she also didn't want to talk about Landon to Jen and Missy, either.

The rustle of leaves behind the girls made them turn.

"What are you guys doing here? Shouldn't you be at breakfast cleanup duty?" Mr. P asked.

"Ms. Merriweather told Jen and me to get Zee and K—" Missy began.

"Yes," Kathi interrupted. "We needed to come get Zee and make sure she's okay." She looked at Zee and smiled.

Zee decided to ignore Kathi's lie. "I'm fine," Zee said cheerfully.

"Then I think everyone needs to get back to work," their teacher told them. "You don't want to be marked down."

Desperate to do something other than talk about Landon with Jen, Missy, and Kathi, Zee said, "I just have to grab something first," and headed to the cabin to finally get a pad.

11

Cabin Fever

efore lunch Zee finally had a chance to do what she'd wanted to do all morning—write in her diary.

| Hi, Diary, |
| I am so confused! I need you to help me sort it |
| all out. |

Things That Really Shouldn't Be Confusing but Are	
What's Confusing?	Why?
Kathi	One minute she seems so confident (and conceited). The next she's just as scared as everyone else (including me).

???	Which is the real Kathi? Does she ever really mean it when she's nice to me, or is it just an act?
Ally	Is what Kathi told me true? Is Ally jealous of me? I can't see why. Did Ally confide in Kathi? Would she really talk about me to her?
Landon	Actually, he's always been confusing.

Ally sat down at the lunch table between Zee and Jasper. "I was just talking to Molly Templeton," she said. "Cabin seven is nearly done with the scavenger hunt list."

"Really?" Kathi sounded surprised. "But we've been working so hard! We *have* to win."

Chloe and Zee looked at each other and rolled their eyes.

"Oh yeah, Kathi, we've *all* been working *really hard*," Ally told her. "I guess *everyone* just needs to work a little harder if we want to win."

Kathi looked farther down the table where Marcus,

Conrad, and Landon were sitting. "Hear that, guys? You need to make more of an effort or we're all going to lose," she chastised them.

Conrad saluted Kathi and said, "Aye, aye, Captain!" while the other three cracked up laughing.

Kathi turned back to the girls. "Boys. So mature."

"Jasper's mature," Ally defended him. "Aren't you, Jasper?"

Jasper looked down and pushed his ground beef hash around on his plate with a fork. "Uh . . . maybe . . . I don't know."

"Oh, come on," Ally said, giving him a little nudge. "You know you are."

"You know you are," Marcus mimicked in a high voice. Once again, the boys started laughing.

"You guys are just jealous," Ally said.

"Of . . . ?" Conrad said.

"Of Jasper," she told him.

"If he's so mature, how come he wears Superman pajamas?" Conrad asked.

Now Jasper looked up. "I don't. I really don't. I wear perfectly respectable flannels."

"Actually, Jasper really does wear flannel," Conrad announced, turning to Jasper. "I was just busting on the girls."

"I think you're embarrassing Jasper," Zee whispered to Ally.

"No, I'm not," Ally said. "Jasper knows I was complimenting him. He doesn't care what the other boys think."

Zee sighed and looked at Jasper. He actually did look fine. So why did Ally's flirty behavior make Zee so uncomfortable?

* * *

Hi, Diary,

Ever since I met Chloe and Jasper, I wanted them to be friends with Ally. But now that we're finally all together, I'm not sure I really want that anymore. I mean, I still want Chloe and Ally to be friends. But it's different with Jasper and Ally.

It really bugs me that Ally is so flirty with Jasper. I'm just not sure <u>why</u> it bothers me. I wouldn't care if she acted that way with Marcus or Conrad. (Okay, I admit it would annoy me if she did it with Landon.)

So why do I care about Jasper?

Maybe if I can get Chloe and Ally to be better friends, Ally won't pay so much attention to Jasper.

Zee

* * *

After lunch, all of the seventh graders met in the main lodge so Mr. P could tell them about the next camp challenge. "We're going to have a cabin decorating contest," he announced.

"Cool beans!" Zee enthused. "I love coming up with decorating ideas. I could spend hours watching home-decorating shows."

"Cabin one can totally win this," Chloe said, turning to Zee.

"I didn't know you were into house decorating, too," Ally said to Chloe.

"This contest is so perfect for Chloe," Zee said. "Her bedroom is amazing. It's an Italian kind of theme, and she even made a really cool mosaic mirror frame out of ceramic pitcher pieces."

Ally half-shrugged. "It's too bad you haven't gotten to see my room in Paris yet," she said. "It's really awesome."

"Oh yeah," Zee said quickly. "I'm sure—just like your room in Brookdale was."

"Zee and I used to redo our bedrooms about once a month," Ally said. "Remember, Zee?"

Zee laughed. "Except for that one summer when we did it once a week."

Mr. P whistled, interrupting the girls' conversation. "The theme is My World," he continued. "You'll have until dinnertime to transform your cabin."

"What do we use—sticks and moss?" Marcus asked.

"Supplies are in the art cabin," Mr. P explained. "After dinner, everyone will tour the student cabins and vote."

Kathi's hand shot up. "That's not fair," she said. "The cabins with the most people will get the most votes."

Mr. P nodded. "Good point. No one can vote for their own cabin." Then he clapped his hands together. "Okay, everyone. Get to work."

"Let's go," Chloe said to the cabin-one girls. "We don't have much time." They hurried out of the lodge to the art cabin.

"Man!" Zee said as she scanned the shelves and tables covered with papers, paints, felt, and other craft supplies.

Other seventh graders crowded in behind them.

"This is just like on *Project Runway* when everyone has to dig through car parts or tear through the grocery store in five minutes," Chloe said. "Who can think that quickly?"

"Yeah, we should pick a theme—fast—so we get the right stuff," Zee suggested.

"You know what would be incredible?" Ally asked. "A Parisian theme. Each corner of the cabin could be an important landmark, and in the center we could re-create the Eiffel Tower."

"That's great!" Chloe began. "But since we're in the woods and the whole trip is about the environment, I think we should do a nature theme. We could create a jungle—with animals from the rain forest."

"No way! It's too obvious," Ally snapped. "We're practically *in* the jungle. Duh."

Chloe looked hurt. And Zee was shocked. Ally had never had a problem expressing her opinion, but she was always nice about it. What was going on?

"Um . . . can I talk to you outside for a second, Ally?" Zee said.

"Why?" Ally asked.

"Uh . . . there's just something I want to show you." Zee grabbed Ally's arm and led her out the door.

As soon as they got outside, Ally turned to Zee. "Which decorating idea do you think is best—mine or Chloe's?" she asked.

"I was hoping I wouldn't have to choose."

"Why? Because Chloe's feelings get hurt so easily?"

"Actually, Chloe's usually really tough," Zee explained. "She just really loves animals."

"Well, I love Paris. That *is* where I live."

Zee scrunched her nose. "Yeah. That's kind of the problem," Zee said slowly.

"What is?" Ally asked suspiciously.

"This is a Brookdale Academy field trip."

Ally's face dropped. "And I'm not a student anymore."

"Right," Zee said, then quickly added, "I mean, it's so great that you got to come, but it seems like if it's between you and Chloe, it might be better for us to do Chloe's idea—since she goes to the school." As soon as the words jumped out of Zee's mouth, she realized how bad they might have sounded to Ally—like Zee was saying Ally didn't belong. But Ally understood that Zee would never mean that, right?

As Ally stared at Zee, Zee couldn't read the expression on her face, so she decided to check. "You understand, right?" Zee said. Her heart pounded as she waited, until Ally finally said, "Okay," then turned to go back into the cabin.

Okay? Zee thought, not exactly sure what that meant. She followed Ally back inside.

"I've been thinking about it," Ally announced to the other girls. "Chloe is right. We should do the rain forest theme."

Ally turned and grinned at Zee, but it wasn't a real grin. It was a *there!-are-you-happy?* grin.

Zee wasn't. Ally stood silent as the other girls designed, planned, and picked out supplies.

Zee brought over two large sheets of green and yellow poster board. "What do you think, Ally?" Zee asked.

"It's all fine," Ally said.

But Zee could tell nothing was fine.

Back at cabin one, each girl volunteered for a job. Chloe said she would work on the animals. Missy wanted to make the trees. Zee said she'd craft the mosses and ferns on the floor of the rain forest. Kathi and Jen must have been scared to hear that their science class might lose the scavenger hunt because even they volunteered to make the vines that would climb up the trees.

"What do you want to do?" Chloe asked Ally.

"You might as well just tell me what you want me to do," Ally said.

"Why?" Chloe asked, sounding a bit aggravated.

"It seems like that's what you want to do."

"I don't know what you're talking about," Chloe said. "All I did was come up with a cabin decorating theme."

"So did I," Ally said.

"Yeah, well . . . we're doing mine," Chloe reminded her.

As the girls got louder and Zee started to panic, Missy

spoke up. "Ally, do you want to help me make the trees over here? I need some ideas."

"Sure," Ally said, cheering up. She didn't even look at Chloe as she moved to where Missy was sitting. "Maybe we could cut the trunks out of paper, then glue leaves and sticks to them to make them look real."

Missy's dark eyes grew wide with excitement. "I *love* that idea. Let's go collect stuff outside."

Zee breathed a silent sigh of relief. "Cool beans! That's a great idea," she said to Ally as the girls got up to leave.

Ally looked at Zee. "Thanks," she said, but Zee thought it sounded a little sarcastic.

As Missy and Zee stepped outside, a twinge of jealousy pinched Zee. Missy had just met Ally, and they were getting along really well. But now after ten years of being friends, something was weird between Ally and Zee.

Hi, Diary,

Does Ally hate me? I know I hurt her feelings, but I didn't mean to. I just want everyone to get along. I think Ally is mad at Chloe, but it's not Chloe's fault.

What if we had done Ally's idea instead of Chloe's? Would Chloe be mad at me? Maybe having a lot of friends means you just can't win.

Zee

The dining hall buzzed with excitement as the seventh graders discussed their transformed cabins.

"What did you guys do to your cabin?" Jen asked Marcus.

"He can't tell you," Conrad said. "Or he'll have to kill you." He high-fived Marcus, Jasper, and Landon, who were laughing.

"That's a horrible thing to say!" Jen protested.

"It's just an expression," Conrad said. "It means 'you'll find out when everyone else does.'"

"Maybe you can get Jasper to tell you," Jen whispered to Zee.

Zee looked at Jasper, who was still laughing. "I don't

think so," Zee said. "After a few days living with those guys, I think he's gone over to the dark side."

Jen gave Zee a nudge with her elbow, then wiggled her eyebrows. "How about Landon?"

Landon was also looking Zee's way. *Ohmylanta!* Zee silently groaned. Had he heard Jen?

Luckily, Ms. Merriweather distracted Landon when she shouted, "All right! Settle down. It's time to tour the cabins." Table by table, the hall quieted. "After you clear your trays, you may go see what your classmates have done. Then come to the main lodge to cast your ballot."

The Beans hurried out of the dining hall. They were dying to see how their cabins compared to the others. The first stop for the cabin-one girls was cabin two. As they rushed up the steps, Kathi pushed her way to the front.

"Oh my gosh!" Kathi squealed. "This is so amazing!" The boys had re-created the Brookdale Academy campus. The garden beds that Chloe and Jasper had planned for their big science project were on one wall. Rain barrels and miniature versions of the school's giant solar tracking panels were on others.

"Are those real carrots?" Missy asked.

Kathi looked nervous. "Do you think they'll beat us?" she wondered out loud.

"I don't know," Zee said. "It's really good." She turned to Chloe. "But so is ours."

"I think this one might be better than ours," Ally said. "Way better."

"We should go look at the others," Zee suggested.

The girls moved from cabin to cabin. Ally had a really positive comment for every transformation but not for her own cabin.

"It's going to be tough for us to beat everyone else," Ally pointed out as the girls walked to the lodge to cast their votes.

Chloe didn't say anything. And Zee didn't know how to respond, either. Why was Ally being so negative? In the end, they had used some of her ideas, and it looked like she was having a good time working with Missy. Something was obviously bothering Ally—something big. And Zee wished she knew what it was so she could fix it.

That evening the light from the campfire bounced off the eager seventh graders' faces. As soon as Mr. P arrived, Conrad shouted, "When are you going to announce that cabin two won the decorating contest?"

The other students laughed.

"I'll announce the winner at the end of the campfire

tonight," Mr. P told him.

"So it's us?" Marcus asked.

"I didn't say that," Mr. P answered.

Conrad looked at his group. "That means it's us," he told them.

Mr. P shook his head and tried to hold back a smile. Zee laughed, too, then realized it was the first time she'd felt happy since the cabin decorating contest had begun.

It was hard to concentrate on that night's singing and games. Even the s'mores weren't enough to distract Zee from the contest.

Finally, Mr. P put her out of her misery. "It's time for the moment you've all been waiting for. And the winner is—"

He paused, holding up the trophy that would go to the winning cabin.

"Hey!" Marcus interrupted. "Isn't that a bowling trophy?"

Mr. P waited for the laughter to die down. "Cabin one."

Zee rocketed off her bench and cheered. Kathi raced up to get the trophy from Mr. P. All the other girls jumped and hugged one another. Except Ally. She stayed seated and smiled weakly.

When Zee turned around, she was surprised to see Ally looking so sad.

Later that night while Kathi read aloud a personality quiz from *Flip* magazine, Zee wrote in her diary. Ally sat quietly on her bunk and faced the wall as she scribbled something in a notebook.

Hi, Diary,

What should I do now? I feel like I'm stuck in the middle. Ally and Chloe aren't getting along, but I want to be friends with both of them. I'm not sure that's possible.

If I had to choose between Ally and Chloe, who would I pick?

Zee stopped writing and looked at Chloe, who was smiling and talking to the other girls, and Ally, who continued to write without looking up. She seemed so lonely. *Flip* was Ally's favorite magazine. But she was acting like she wasn't interested in the quiz.

> *Maybe Ally has already chosen not to be my friend.*
>
> *Zee*

At the rehearsal for the talent show the next day, Zee's group had borrowed props from other campers and gotten permission to use a few items from the camp's lost and found. Ally giggled and smiled as she slicked back Jasper's hair with gel.

Zee was glad that Ally hadn't abandoned the skit, although she suspected that was only because of Jasper.

"Mr. P!" Ally shouted to the teacher. "Come show Jasper how to move like a real rock star."

"You must have mistaken *me* for a real rock star," Mr. P joked.

"Ha ha," Ally said sarcastically. "Zee told me that you used to be in a band that toured Europe."

"And now he has a new band," Jasper told Ally. "It's called the Crew."

"Please," Ally pleaded with Mr. P.

"Okay," Mr. P agreed. He positioned Jasper's hands on his bass. He showed Jasper how to hang his head and bob it up and down in time to the music. Then he told Jasper to slide his right foot out in front of his body and tap his toes to keep the beat.

Ally clapped her hands excitedly. "Doesn't he look awesome?" she asked Zee and Chloe. Zee was happy to see Ally in such a good mood—and thrilled that Ally didn't seem mad anymore.

Outlined by the turned-up collar of a black leather jacket, Jasper's face turned red. Zee couldn't believe Jasper's transformation. He looked really good—like himself but also like someone completely new.

"Okay, guys," Ally announced once Jasper had his part figured out. "I worked on the final choreography last night."

Cool beans! Zee thought. *That's what she was writing in her notebook!*

"I was thinking that Jasper could start out offstage," Ally began, standing straight. "The girls could start out in a row. Zee, you stand here." She gestured to a spot on her left, then her right. "And, Chloe, you stand here."

Zee and Chloe took their positions. Then Ally demonstrated the first few dance moves.

"Awesome!" Chloe said. "Let's try it."

Ally counted off a beat, and the three girls stepped

and turned together as though they'd been practicing for a week.

Zee smiled as she looked at her friends. It was great to have everyone back together again.

"What's next?" Zee asked.

Ally took the girls through a few more steps. "Then Jasper comes up." She waved him onto the stage. "He walks up to me and taps me on the shoulder. Of course, when I see him, I go completely crazy. Then I calm down and go like this." Ally took three steps toward Jasper, snapping to the beat. "And here's what you do, Jasper." She showed Jasper how to shimmy down, then cross his legs and spin around.

"Brilliant!" Jasper exclaimed.

"What about us?" Chloe asked. "What do we do while you and Jasper are dancing?"

"Oh, right," Ally said. "You go to the back of the stage. Zee will play her guitar, and you can sing backup, Chloe."

"Backup?" Chloe sounded annoyed.

Ally nodded. "For now."

Zee looked nervously at Chloe. "Umm . . . should Chloe and I just practice the music while you guys work on this part of the dance routine?" Zee asked Ally.

"Yeah," Ally said. "That's a good idea."

Zee hurried Chloe off to the side and pulled her guitar out of its case.

"Why don't you start out with a solo," Zee suggested. "I'll play along and join in singing on the second verse."

Chloe's face beamed. "That's so nice. Thanks." Zee strummed her guitar as Chloe sang, hoping Chloe would forget about Ally and the dance routine.

But when the girls finished the song, Chloe glared at Ally, who was in the midst of a flirty walk across the stage.

"When are we going to get a chance to dance?" Chloe asked.

"Ally said we'd do it later," Zee reminded her.

"I'm not so sure about that. The group doesn't get very much time to perform. This part is going to take it all up."

Finally, Ally and Jasper took a break.

"I have a suggestion," Chloe said in a forceful voice.

Uh-oh, Zee thought. A funny feeling crept through her.

"What?" Ally asked Chloe suspiciously.

"I think that maybe we should take turns so that everyone has a chance to be out front," Chloe explained.

"That doesn't make sense," Ally said. "The dance is kind of like a skit with characters. I think the story could get too confusing with too many leads."

"Confusing to who?" Chloe asked.

"To the audience," Ally told her. "But don't worry. I have some really cool moves for you guys to do behind Jasper and me."

"I think the audience will be able to figure the story out," Chloe said.

"I did all the work," Ally pointed out. "You didn't do anything."

"You didn't give me—or Zee—a chance," Chloe protested.

Ally looked at Zee. Zee felt stuck between her two closest friends. "I don't care if I get a bigger role," Zee said.

"See?" Ally said to Chloe, then gave Zee a smile.

Chloe looked hurt.

"But it does seem fair to trade off if Chloe doesn't feel like she's getting a turn," Zee continued. "After all, she doesn't even have an instrument to play."

"The cabin decoration was Chloe's idea," Ally said. "This is my idea."

"But everyone had an equal part in the cabin decorating—and the trophy belongs to all of us," Zee responded.

"Well, Zee, it's pretty clear whose side you're on!" Ally said loudly. "What do you think, Jasper?"

Jasper nervously looked at the ground and shrugged. "I think you guys should work it out."

The girls started talking at once, shouting over one another. No one could hear what anyone was saying, until Ally shouted, "I quit!"

"You can't quit," Zee pleaded. "This was your idea." Zee was stunned. Everything was falling apart.

"Not anymore," Ally answered.

"What about our grade?" Zee asked. "All the seventh graders are supposed to perform."

"Remember? I'm not a Brookdale Academy student anymore," Ally said. Then she stormed off.

✳ ⚘12 ✳

<u>Just a Crutch</u>

Hi, Diary,

I felt weird around Ally all day. I want to make up with her, but she's officially not speaking to me. She's barely even looking at me. And now she won't talk to Jasper because he's hanging out with me so much, and she'd have to come near me to talk to him. The only person she will talk to is Missy.

Ally may be done being my friend, but I'm not done being hers. I'm sure there's a way to be friends with her and Chloe. I just have to figure out how.

Zee

As Zee entered the dining hall for dinner, she noticed Ally was the last person in line for food. Perfect! This was Zee's chance to make up with her!

Zee rushed to get behind her. "Hi," she said.

Ally spun around with a smile on her face. Zee could feel her whole body sigh with relief.

Then Ally's smile became a frown. "Oh, I thought you were Missy," she said, and stepped out of the line. "I think I'll go find her."

Zee got her food and sat down, then waited for Ally to do the same. When Ally sat next to Missy, Zee slid into the empty spot beside her at the table. But Ally turned away from Zee and joined in Missy and Kathi's conversation.

"What are you guys talking about?" Zee asked.

"Café Lulu in Paris," Kathi said. "We go there every time we visit. They have awesome pastries. Have you ever been?"

"No," Zee told her. "I've never been to Paris."

Kathi looked at Zee as if she had a zit right between her eyeballs. "Really?" Kathi said. "I didn't know there actually was anyone who had never been to Paris. I guess you were busy visiting other parts of France?"

"No, I've never been to France."

"Oh," Kathi said, then turned back to Ally and Missy. "Have you ever had the tarts? Mmmm. They're my favorite."

It was no use. Zee was on the outside. Being Ally's BFF again would just have to wait. Zee just hoped she wouldn't have to wait forever.

Hi, Diary,

I can't remember ever not being best friends with Ally. I know I have other friends, but that's what started the problem. I want Ally back.

The worst part is, she's supposed to live with my family next week. I want her there, but she might not want to stay with me.

My Questions for Ally
(If I could get her to talk to me to answer them)

1. Are you going to give me the silent treatment next week, too? In my own house?

2. Will you sleep in my room?

3. Will you talk to my parents?

4. Will it be the longest week of my life?

Zee

* * *

Zee and Chloe studied the evening work assignments on the cabin door.

"Firewood," Zee read out loud. "I'm supposed to do it with Ally, but she switched assignments with one of the boys in cabin two so she could be with Missy. What do you have?" she asked Chloe.

"Yay! S'mores," Chloe told her. "I hope I don't end up eating all the chocolate!"

"Save some for me," Zee said.

As Zee headed down the path toward the campfire area to start collecting wood, a voice called out behind her. "Zee!"

Zee turned around and stopped. It was Landon! Her heart pounded as she repeated in her head, *No big deal—he's just a friend*, and he hurried to catch up.

"Hey!" Landon said once he'd reached Zee. "I didn't expect to see you on firewood duty, too."

"Why?" Zee asked.

"Because Ally switched jobs with me. I figured it was because she wanted to have the same job as you."

"No," Zee said, and sighed. "It's the opposite. She's not talking to me right now."

"Why not?"

"I'm not exactly sure," Zee said. "Having her back in Brookdale is harder than I thought it would be. She's not really acting like herself."

"How's she acting?"

"Kind of jealous."

"Of you?"

"Sort of." Zee paused. "Of my friendship with Chloe—and Jasper."

"I know how she feels."

"You do?"

"I'm jealous of Jasper, too."

"Why?"

"He gets to hang out with you a lot," Landon told her. By now, he and Zee had reached the campfire area.

"Well, yeah, because we're really good friends."

Landon took one step closer to Zee and leaned forward. His face was right next to hers. Zee's heart sped up. Then Landon kissed her! It happened so quickly, Zee couldn't believe it.

Suddenly, Zee's legs wobbled. "I thought we were just friends," she said.

"Is that what you want?" Landon asked.

No way! Zee thought. But for some reason, she couldn't get the words out. Something was holding her back.

"I don't know," she finally said.

"Well, we better get the wood to the campfire," Landon said, looking embarrassed. He hurried to collect an armful of sticks and rushed off.

Zee looked around. She had come to camp with three best friends, but now she was all alone—after the most amazing moment of her life. Her first kiss!

Hi, Diary,
Landon kissed me! A real kiss. On the lips! I really want to tell Ally, but I'm afraid she might not care. Who can I tell?

Person	Pro	Con
Chloe	She's my best girl friend.	She knows I promised my parents that Landon and I are just friends.
Kathi	We're GWP's together.	She thinks he's too immature for me.
Jasper	He's my best boy friend.	He hates Landon. (Why can't they get along!?)
Missy	She's really nice.	We're not good enough friends yet.
Jen	OMG! She would care and would want to know!	That's too weird.

This was supposed to be one of the best weeks of my life. Me and Ally—just like old times. Instead, my BFF hates me. How can I fix this—without losing my other friends?

Zee

Thunk. Thunk. Thunk. The wall next to Zee's head vibrated. She looked at her cabin mates, all sound asleep. *Thunk. Thunk. Thunk.* Zee's heart started pounding.

"My leg." A deep, rough voice came from the other side of the cabin wall. The Mountain Man was inches away from Zee!

The ground crackled as the Mountain Man walked—toward the cabin door! "Arroo. Ugha." The noises didn't sound human anymore, and Zee's whole body shook at the thought of what might happen when she finally came face-to-face with this stranger. But she didn't intend to find out. She opened her mouth to scream.

"Who's out there?" Mr. P's voice interrupted Zee.

There was no response. Zee could hear the Mountain Man run away.

Ohmylanta! Zee thought. What if he hadn't been awake? What if the Mountain Man had actually come into the cabin?

Of course, now Zee couldn't sleep. The Mountain Man was still out there—and Mr. P might be sleeping the next time he attacked.

Zee got out of bed and looked at Ally sleeping soundly on the bunk above. Then she tiptoed to Chloe. *Pssst!* She quietly tried to wake her. Chloe didn't stir.

"Chloe!" Zee loudly whispered in her ear. Chloe rolled over to her other side and faced the wall away from Zee. Zee reached up and gave her a little shake. "Chloe!"

Chloe's eyes popped open. "What?" She sat up straight.

"The Mountain Man was here," Zee told her friend in a quiet voice.

"How do you know it was the Mountain Man?"

"I think he's looking for his leg."

"We don't have it!" Chloe was starting to sound angry.

"That's not what he thinks."

"Let's go check," Chloe said. She slipped out of her sleeping bag and grabbed her flashlight.

"Okay, but we better not wake anyone else," Zee said. "I think Mr. P would be really angry this time."

The girls quietly moved across the cabin floor so they wouldn't wake the others. Chloe walked so close behind Zee, they were practically one person. Zee carefully pushed open the door and looked around. In the dark, they couldn't see much. Which was a relief. As long as the Mountain Man wasn't nearby, Zee was happy. They took a few steps forward.

Before Zee knew what was happening, she'd fallen to the ground.

"What happened?" Chloe asked, panicked.

"I tripped over something."

"Are you all right?"

Zee got up and brushed herself off. "I'm fine. What was that?"

Chloe shined her light on the forest floor. At first, all she saw was the usual—leaves, twigs, and pinecones. Then she found something that didn't belong in the woods—a crutch.

The light danced around as Chloe's hand started shaking. "How did that get here?" she asked loudly.

Zee took a step back—as Mr. P hurried out of his cabin. "What's going on?" he shouted. Zee didn't need to see his face to know he was angry.

"We heard . . . uh . . . something," Zee explained.

"What?" Mr. P asked impatiently. Up close, Zee could see that he was wearing a black Yes No concert T-shirt and flannel pajamas. Raccoon circles surrounded his sleepy eyes, and his hair stuck up every which way.

Chloe glanced down at the crutch. "That's what we were trying to figure out."

"This is your second warning this week," Mr. P told them. "I think we might have to take some disciplinary action."

"But someone banged against the wall of the cabin and woke me up," Zee defended herself.

"Really?" Mr. P sounded concerned. "Who?"

Zee decided that she probably shouldn't try to explain

that a hairy one-legged mountain creature in search of his missing limb had interrupted her sleep. Mr. P was a really cool teacher, but without more evidence, he might not be ready to hear the truth.

"Um . . . I don't know," Zee told him.

"We'll talk about this when we get back to school next week—as long as I don't see you out here again." Mr. P rubbed his head and turned to go.

Chloe quickly bent down and picked up the crutch. Then the girls carefully went back up the cabin steps.

13

Man-Oh-Man

The next morning, all the seventh graders met in the lodge for announcements. As she waited, Zee watched the door. She had saved a seat for Ally—just in case. Chloe sat on the other side of her next to Jasper.

When other kids tried to sit in the empty seat, Zee politely explained, "I'm saving that for someone."

But when Ally arrived with Missy, they sat at the far end of the row. Zee was sure Ally saw her—even though Ally tried to make it look as though she didn't.

Marcus, Conrad, and Landon came in together.

Landon smiled and waved at Zee. As Marcus and Conrad went to sit by Ally and Missy, Landon came over to Zee.

"Can I sit here?" he asked.

At first, Zee couldn't answer. Didn't Landon feel weird about the kiss? Her heart felt like it was planning an escape—right through her ribs.

Jasper spoke for Zee. "She's saving that seat."

Wait! No! Zee thought. *That's not what I want to say!* She took a deep breath to calm herself down, then said, "Actually, you can sit there."

Jasper looked shocked. "You were saving it for Landon?" he asked.

"Uh . . . um . . . ," Zee said.

"Thanks!" Landon said, ignoring Jasper, to Zee's relief.

With Landon next to her, Zee expected her face to turn red and her heart to start pounding again. She looked down at her hands to see if they were shaking.

Instead, Zee was surprised that she felt completely normal. After the kiss, Zee expected everything to change. But it was like her period. On the outside she wasn't different at all.

In fact, the only person who seemed to be noticing that something out of the ordinary was happening was Jasper.

And Ally. When Zee looked at her, she looked away.

"Okay, everyone, just a couple of quick announcements before we break for breakfast," Mr. P said. "Please have all of your belongings packed before the talent show this afternoon. We're going to leave as soon as it's over."

As quickly as Zee's heart had risen when Landon sat next to her, it sank as she thought about performing in the talent show without Ally. Zee had really tried to make things right with Ally, but now there was nothing more she could do.

"Also—" Mr. P continued, pointing to the door in the back of the room marked INFIRMARY, "the nurse reported that a crutch is missing from her office. She accidentally left it leaning against a tree near cabin fifteen. So if you find it, please return it to her. Okay, that's all."

A crutch? Zee thought. She and Chloe looked at each other and knew they were thinking the same thing. "That's

the crutch we found!" they said together.

"But how did it get all the way over from cabin fifteen to our cabin?" Chloe wondered out loud.

"And why did whoever brought it over pound on the cabin and grumble about his leg?"

Then the girls heard a sudden burst of laughter. They looked around. At the other end of the row, Conrad and Marcus were high-fiving each other as they hurried toward Zee and Chloe. Landon doubled over laughing and Jasper joined in.

"Has anybody seen a crutch?" Conrad asked.

"Or a leg?" Marcus added.

"Yeah, if you find a leg, you should probably give that to the nurse, too," Conrad agreed.

"Very funny," Chloe said, giving Marcus a shove.

"*You* were the Mountain Man this whole time!" Zee accused.

"Yup," Conrad confirmed.

"We weren't sure if you'd fall for it, but it was actually way too easy," Marcus put in.

"I don't get it," Zee said, still trying to put the prank to-gether. "What about when you were dragged in the woods?"

"That's right!" Chloe said. "We saw the piece of ripped shirt stuck to the tree branch."

"Thanks to the lost and found," Conrad explained. "They've got all sorts of cool stuff in there."

"That doesn't make sense. I know I saw something huge run into the woods," Zee reminded the boys. "You're not that tall."

Conrad climbed onto a chair, then onto Marcus's shoulders. "Something about this tall?" Marcus asked.

Chloe stamped her foot and shook her head. "I can't believe you tricked us!"

"Actually, we had no idea it would be so easy," Conrad said.

The teasing continued through breakfast. "Aaaaa! It's the Mountain Man!" Marcus said in a high-pitched voice.

"Oh, he's so scary," Conrad joined in.

"And hairy," Marcus added.

"I thought you were going to tell Mr. P everything last night," Conrad went on. "That would have been hilarious."

By now, all of the Beans

knew about the boys' trick and were laughing.

"Okay. Okay," Zee said when she stopped. "You can stop talking about it now."

Secretly, though, Zee wished Ally would say something—even if it were just "I told you so." Instead she continued to pretend that she didn't even know Zee was there.

Then Zee realized that Jasper was laughing loudest of all. She looked at him suspiciously. "Did you know what they were up to?" she asked.

"Give me back my leg," Jasper said in a weird voice with a strange accent.

"How could you make Jasper do that?" Chloe accused Conrad and Marcus.

"Make him do it?" Conrad said. "It was his idea!"

Zee's mouth dropped open. "I thought you were my friend!" she said.

"I am," Jasper told her. "But I'm also friends with my cabin mates." He looked in Marcus and Conrad's direction, but Zee noticed he avoided looking at Landon. "Everyone needs lots of friends."

Of course! Jasper was right. He didn't have to choose between Zee and Chloe and the boys. They could all be friends.

Hi, Diary,

I shouldn't feel bad about having more than one friend—no matter how long I've been BFFs with Ally. Now that Ally lives in France, I need other people. And I can't just dump them when Ally comes to town. Still, she'll always be my BFF—even if Chloe and Jasper are my best friends, too.

But Ally needs to know that. She was probably feeling totally weird about coming back to Brookdale. Instead of everything being the same, there were a lot of changes—Chloe, Jasper, Missy, Mr. P, the Beans. I was trying so hard to make everything fit together, but I ended up making it fall apart.

Now I'm going to fix it.

Zee

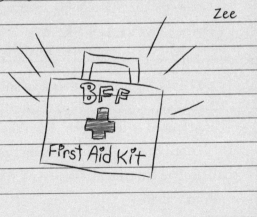

* * *

Zee got her chance to make things right with Ally later that morning when they both finally got their computer time.

 E-ZEE: Hi.

Zee started to send an IM to Ally; then she stopped herself. *No, that's not right,* she thought. "Hi" was enough to start a chat under normal circumstances, but these weren't normal circumstances. Zee had much more to say. Zee might have only one shot to get Ally back. She hit the delete key and tried again.

 E-ZEE: I miss u. I am really sorry about taking C's side w/ the cabin decorating. I didn't mean 2 hurt ur feelings—b/c u r my BFF 4ever!

 E-ZEE: P.S. will u pls b in the talent show??

Zee looked at the screen. Then she looked at her hands, which until that moment she hadn't realized were actually shaking. She sent the message. And waited.

And waited.

Zee peered over at Ally. Did she get the IM? Did she read

it? Would she respond? As she waited for a reply, Zee tried to type an email to her parents and Adam, but it was just too hard. How could she tell them about everything that had happened? Zee looked at the computer clock. *Ohmylanta!* she silently groaned. Only a minute had passed. *How is that possible?* Zee wondered. It seemed more like fifteen. Maybe Ally had single-handedly figured out a way to make time stand still just to torture Zee. Zee couldn't blame her.

Maybe the computer's frozen, Zee thought. She hit a few keys to make sure everything was working. It was.

Sitting and waiting was just too much for Zee. The IM might never come. She moved her cursor across the page to log out at the top of the screen, ready to sign off for the day.

Just as she was about to click on the mouse, a response popped up.

Ohmy-ohmy-lanta! Zee thought. *Of course!* Ally took so long because she was writing a response.

 SPARKLEGRRL: I miss u 2!!!! I thought I was getting in the way & u didn't want me around anymore. I kinda freaked out about the cabins. I know u r dying 2 c paris & I wanted 2 make it 4 u. when u picked c's idea

over mine, I was kinda embarrassed.
u have so many new people in ur life
now. I got worried that maybe it
wasn't just c's idea u were picking.
I thought u were choosing her over
me. I figured u didn't want 2 tell me
u had a new BFF.

This time Zee really did log off. Then she rushed over to
Ally, who jumped out of her seat. The girls hugged.

14
Cabin One's Revenge

"I'm so sorry!" Ally said. "You must think I'm completely horrible."

"No way!" Zee said. "I wanted you to feel like you were still part of the group. And I wanted my new friends to know that they were really important to me, too. I thought it was my job to keep everyone happy."

"Well, that is what makes you Zee," Ally reminded her.

"Instead I ended up miserable without you," Zee added.

"Yeah, that part of the plan didn't work out so well," Ally said. Which made Zee crack up. Which made Ally crack up. Just like they used to laugh together.

As the girls stood there, Chloe entered the lodge with

the Mountain Man crutch.

"Don't remind me," Zee said. "I can't believe we fell for the boys' stupid prank."

Chloe rolled her eyes. "We should have listened to Ally," Chloe said. "She never believed he was real."

"Are you kidding?" Ally said. "Maybe I didn't believe it at first, but by the end, I was totally with you guys."

"Unfortunately, the Mountain Man wasn't the only monster the boys created," Chloe went on.

"He wasn't?" Zee asked.

"No, they also made a new version of Jasper. He won't stop talking about how 'brilliant' the plan was," Chloe said, impersonating Jasper's accent.

"Too bad we can't get them back," Zee said.

"That's it!" Ally said.

"What?" Chloe and Zee asked at once.

"We can get them back," Ally told them.

"How?" Zee asked. "We're going home this evening."

"That gives us the rest of the day to plan," Ally said. "Plus, you're forgetting about the fact that your families are coming *here*."

Zee looked at her friend suspiciously. "What do they have to do with it?"

"Not *them*—just Adam."

Chloe perked up. "Tell us!"

The three girls huddled together to talk about Ally's plan. Then they sent Adam an email to tell him what he needed to do to help them.

The Brookdale Academy families arrived to join the campers for dinner before the talent show. Zee, Ally, and Chloe rushed over to Adam while Mr. and Mrs. Carmichael talked to Chloe's parents.

"Did you bring the supplies?" Zee asked her brother.

Adam unzipped his backpack and showed the girls his stash.

"Okay," Ally said. "While we're eating, you need to arrange everything in cabin two."

"Won't Mom and Dad notice I'm missing?" Adam asked.

"Don't worry," Zee assured him. "I'll take care of them."

As Adam went off to set the trap, Zee, Chloe, and Ally went over to the Carmichaels and Lawrence-Johnsons.

"Where's Adam off to?" Zee's mother asked.

"There's something I want to tell you, Mom." Zee took her mother's arm and began to lead her away. "You guys go ahead and start eating," Zee told the rest of the group.

"Oh . . . uh . . . okay, honey," Mrs. Carmichael said. The way Zee was dragging her away, however, made it clear she didn't have much choice. Ally and Chloe led Mr. Carmichael and the Lawrence-Johnsons toward the serving line.

"What is it, Zee?" Mrs. Carmichael asked when they were safely out of earshot of the other campers.

"Guess what I got this week?" Zee teased.

"Poison ivy?" her mother asked. "Oh, I was worried about that. I hope the nurse—"

"No, Mom," Zee interrupted. "It's not poison ivy."

"What is it, then?"

Zee leaned closer. "My period," she whispered.

Mrs. Carmichael instantly squeezed Zee in a hug. "That's so wonderful!" Then she stepped back. "Are you okay? I mean, you didn't have any supplies with you."

"I'm fine," Zee assured her. "Kathi helped me out."

"That was nice of her," Mrs. Carmichael said. "We'll have to make sure you have your own now that you're all grown up." She wiped at a tear in the corner of her eye.

"Mom," Zee said. "It's not that big a deal." She wanted to tell her mother about the really big deal—the kiss with Landon—but she figured that she'd told her enough big news for the moment. Plus, she needed to stop the waterworks before her mother completely embarrassed her.

Then out of the corner of her eye, Zee watched her brother come through the lodge doors. When she glanced his way, he gave her a thumbs-up. Zee could see that his backpack was no longer full.

"I'm hungry," Zee said to her mother. "We should eat."

"Good idea," Mrs. Carmichael said, turning around. "Oh, there's Adam. He must have gone to the bathroom."

At the end of the meal, Mr. P stood up. "Attention, campers and seventh-grade families," he shouted so everyone could hear him. "It's time for the students to get ready for the talent show. Our guests can find their seats at the outdoor stage area while the performers prepare in their cabins."

Zee hopped out of her seat. "Bye, Mom and Dad," she said. "Gotta go!"

"Yeah, see you later," Ally added.

"Where are you girls going in such a rush?" Mr. Carmichael asked.

"We have to change into our costumes," Chloe explained as she followed the other two. But the three girls didn't head to the cabin right away. Instead they found Missy, Kathi, and Jen.

"Hurry!" Zee told the other three girls. "We've got a surprise for you."

"What?" Kathi asked suspiciously.

"Trust me," Zee said. "You will not want to miss this."

"Excellent!" Missy said, moving faster.

That was all Kathi needed. She wasn't going to let Missy be part of the surprise without her.

The girls rushed to their cabin, but Zee stopped them at the door. "Don't go in yet," she explained. "The surprise is out here."

They waited anxiously for the cabin-two boys to come. Finally, the boys arrived—with Adam.

"What are you guys waiting for?" Conrad asked when he saw them standing outside. "The Mountain Man?"

"Ha ha!" Chloe said.

"We were just thanking Adam for giving us the idea in the first place," Marcus said as the group continued to walk by.

Zee laughed and Ally whispered to Chloe, "They won't be thanking Adam in a minute."

Suddenly, one by one, Marcus, Conrad, Landon, and Jasper shot out of cabin two.

"Aaaaaaa!" they screamed in unison.

"They're all over the place!" Conrad yelled.

"I think one is still on me!" Marcus added.

"Crikey!" Jasper held on to his arm as he ran. "I think one bit me!"

The boys scrambled in all directions, screaming louder than Zee had ever heard anyone scream.

Eventually Adam appeared at the door to cabin two. The girls rushed to him.

"What did you do?" Missy shouted excitedly.

"What a bunch of immature babies!" Kathi said.

Jen followed behind. "I have got to see this."

"Just don't freak out," Adam said as they entered the cabin. "It's all fake."

Like a carpet over the wooden floor, snakes were everywhere.

Zee scooped down to pick one up. "Rubber," she said, holding it out to show everyone.

"That actually went much better than I'd planned," Ally said.

"That's because I made it better," Adam told them. "I rigged a sheet up to the ceiling. When the boys opened the door, it pulled the sheet over, and the snakes came tumbling down on top of them."

"That's awesome!" Chloe cheered.

"I have to admit, it is cool beans," Zee said. "But don't let it go to your head."

"I know," Adam said, patting her on the shoulder. "I know."

Zee rolled her eyes. "Stop doing that before I take back the compliment."

"You can't. I have witnesses." Adam began collecting his snakes and putting them in his backpack. "Now excuse me while I clean up. I think I might need these again this week." He smiled deviously at Zee and Ally.

"Ohmylanta!" Zee groaned. "Now *I've* created a monster."

Show Time

The talent show was amazing. All the seventh graders showed off their skills. Gymnasts tumbled and flipped. A juggler caught balls while balancing a plate on a stick. And a baton twirler threw her baton so high, it looked like it might never come back down. There were ballet and hip-hop dancers, synchronized Hula-hoops, and rappers.

Kathi's practice paid off. She and Missy both played incredibly well and sounded like a team. Marcus, Landon, Conrad, and Jen's comedy routine had Zee laughing so hard, she was afraid her sides might hurt too much to do her own act.

When Zee, Chloe, Jasper, and of course, Ally, did perform, they stole the show. Each girl took a turn singing a solo, and Zee and Ally played a duet while Chloe danced across the stage. Everyone had a chance to shine.

Thanks to the fact that Zee had packed so many extra clothes, she was able to put together coordinated outfits—T-shirts with sequins and capri pants. Each girl also had a different colored scarf twisted around her hair.

"Forever fabulous. That's what you'll be," the trio belted out the lyrics. "Forever fabulous. Try it and see."

Zee had even changed the words just a little for the occasion. And that was the part they sang the loudest. "We're four best friends—there for each other. Four best friends—in it together."

But it was Jasper's new style that really wowed the audience. He snarled his lip and jerked his head back while the girls circled and swooned.

By the end, Ally wasn't the only one who had a crush on him. Most of the seventh-grade girls were finding any excuse to talk to him. Zee thought he might die from all of the attention. He awkwardly looked at the ground and shuffled his feet in the dirt.

Zee couldn't believe it when two guys pulled up to the camp on motorcycles. Guitars were strapped to their bodies. As soon as they took off their helmets, Zee recognized them—the other members of Mr. P's band, the Crew. When

all the kids were finished performing, they got onstage and played a song called "Campers' Complaints" that Mr. P had written just for the occasion.

"No text. What next?" the men sang as Zee and her friends smiled sheepishly. "Kitchen crew? I've got the flu."

As the seventh graders listened and laughed, Ally whispered in Zee's ear. "The Beans should all play a song together."

"That's a great idea!" Zee agreed. "Which one?"

"How about another one you wrote?" Ally suggested.

"Only if you'll perform with us," Zee told her.

"Me?"

"You have your flute and know all the words to my songs," Zee reminded her. "And you're practically a member of the band anyway."

Ally smiled. "Deal!"

"Cool beans!" Zee said.

"Very cool Beans!" Ally agreed.

The girls whispered the idea to the other band members. Everyone thought it was a great idea.

As soon as the Crew finished playing, the Beans hurried onstage.

Mr. P didn't have to ask what was going on. "Ladies and gentlemen," he announced over the applause for his

performance. "The Beans!"

"This song is called 'Two of a Kind,'" Zee said. Then she turned to Ally and nodded.

"One, two, three, four," Ally counted off. And the Beans began to play. Ally sounded as though she had been practicing with the band since the beginning of the school year. The violins traded off the melody with her flute. Jasper played bass and Zee played her guitar while Marcus took keyboards. Jen and Landon played along on the percussion instruments they'd used for the drum circle. And Conrad's saxophone rang out across the campgrounds.

Without her cello, Chloe sang lead. She'd never sounded better than she did that day. No one did. When Chloe got to the last line of the song, instead of singing, "We're two of a kind," she changed the words to "We're eight of a kind." All of the Beans sang along, repeating the line over and over.

After the clapping died down and the Beans cleared the stage, Ms. Merriweather took her place on it. "Before we say good-bye, I want to announce the winner of the scavenger hunt," she said in a loud voice.

The Beans nervously waited. Zee crossed her fingers.

"The class that found the most items is"—the science teacher paused dramatically—"first period." A cheer went up from the left side of the stage and a small group of parents in the audience.

Even though they'd lost, the Beans clapped along, too. Except for one member of the band. "No fair!" Kathi said loudly.

Zee, Chloe, and Ally looked at one another and rolled their eyes.

But Zee knew Kathi wasn't the real reason they'd lost. She was certain that they would have won if they had worked as a team sooner. Still, in the end, they'd gotten more than a science lesson that week. They'd learned about friendship, too.

As Zee, Chloe, and Ally walked back to cabin one to get their luggage, Zee suddenly stopped in her tracks. "I can't believe it!"

"What?" Chloe asked, turning around.

Ally stopped, too. "Are you upset about losing the scavenger hunt?"

"That's not it," Zee said. "I forgot to tell you the big news."

Chloe and Ally looked at each other. "Four-one-one please," Ally said.

"Yeah, spill," Chloe commanded.

Zee looked around to make sure no one else was listening. "Guess who kissed me yesterday!"

Ally's mouth dropped open. "No. Way."

"Landon?" Chloe asked. Zee nodded as the girls started moving down the path again. "And you kept it from us the whole day?"

"I've been dying to tell you," Zee assured them.

"Are you going to write your initials together on the cabin wall?" Ally asked.

"Did you write yours and Jacques's?" Zee replied

"But of course," Ally said with a fake French accent.

Chloe bit her lip. "So are you going to tell Jasper?" she asked.

"Umm . . . no," Zee said, wrinkling her nose. "Should I? It feels kind of weird."

By now the girls had almost reached their cabin. "I

wouldn't worry about it," Chloe said. She pointed to the crowd outside of cabin two. Adoring seventh-grade girls had surrounded Jasper as he looked at the ground and nervously shoved his hands in his pockets.

"Think we should save him?" Ally asked.

Zee watched as a huge smile spread across Jasper's face. "I don't really think he wants us to."

16

BFFs

BFFs 4 ever!!!

Hi, Diary,

Camp was the best week of my life. But I admit that I'm happy to be back in my comfy bed with real food and my mom and dad spoiling me.

How lucky can you get? Even though we lost the scavenger hunt, I feel like a winner. All the Beans do. Mr. P says we might be ready to play outside of school events soon. Which would be totally awesome.

I hope Ally—and Chloe and Jasper—knows that no matter what, we will always be friends.

Zee

* * *

On Saturday, Zee and Ally invited Chloe and Jasper to hang out at Zee's house. Missy came, too, since Ally had gotten to be such good friends with her at camp.

Mrs. Carmichael put out a tray of pita chips and dips, fruit, and tiny sandwiches. Zee and her friends devoured the snacks while they played Wii and talked about their week.

"Oh my gosh!" Missy scrunched up her face. "Do you remember Wednesday's lunch? What *was* that?"

"I don't know," Ally said, "but they paid a guy in second period to put it in his milk glass and drink it."

"Ewww," Chloe and Zee groaned.

"Jasper, would you ever do anything that gross?" Zee asked him.

"Pffft tmnt glp," Jasper responded. Nobody liked Mrs. Carmichael's snack trays more than he did. His mouth wasn't empty until the tray was empty.

"Oh, I'm going to miss you guys so much when I have to go back to France," Ally told them.

"You still have another week in Brookdale, though," Missy reminded her.

"I never thought I'd actually want to go to school on my

vacation, but since that's the only way I'll get to hang out with you guys, I'm going to do it."

"And after that, we'll just email and IM you constantly," Missy said.

"Except French time is nine hours ahead of L.A. time. Sometimes I'm asleep when you're awake."

Jasper swallowed his mouthful of food. "I have the same problem with my friends in England."

"What do you do?" Zee asked.

"I'm working on a solution now," Jasper said. "I'll let you know if I figure it out."

"Well, I think we should definitely do this again soon," Chloe said.

Ally nodded. "In France!"

"What's it like to kiss Landon?" Ally asked Zee when they were getting ready for bed that night.

"I really don't know," Zee said.

"What?"

"I was so shocked that it even happened, I don't remember it!"

Ally squirted toothpaste on her toothbrush. "Are you boyfriend and girlfriend now?"

"I'm not sure," Zee said, hesitating.

"What do you mean?" Ally asked.

"Well, I thought that that's what I really wanted. I've had a crush on Landon since we were little. But now I'm just not sure."

"Really?"

"Yeah. Is that weird?" Zee asked. "I mean, I thought it would be cool to have a boyfriend with you."

Ally shook her head. "You shouldn't want a boyfriend just because I have one, and you shouldn't have one if you don't want one."

"I don't know what I want," Zee told her.

"Then you should wait to decide."

"You're right," Zee said, turning the water on to wash her face.

"Now you have to tell me—what's it like to get your period?" Ally asked Zee.

"Mostly, it doesn't feel different—except for the cramps."

Ally wrinkled her nose. "At least now you'll know you're not sick."

"Yeah, and Mom says I might not even get them every time."

"I am definitely going to call you right away when I get mine," Ally told Zee.

"You better!"

Before the girls turned out the lights, Zee logged on to her email. There was a new message from Landon!

Hi, Zee,
Do u like me? B/c I know I like u. u r so funny & nice. I don't feel weird about our kiss. I want to be more than friends.
wb & tell me if u do 2.
Landon

Zee hit reply and put her fingers on the keyboard. No words came out of her fingertips. Nothing had changed since she'd talked to Ally. She was still confused. Her answer to Landon would have to wait until she was sure.

Then Zee picked up her diary and started to write her next song.

"Camp Kiss"

Online Glossary

2	to; two; too
4	for
b	be
b/c	because
BFF	best friend forever
c	see
OMG	Oh my God
pls	please
r	are
u	you
ur	your
wb	write back

Acknowledgments

I must first say a big thank-you to Mackenzie's godmothers, Catherine Onder and Tara Weikum. Special thanks to my entire HarperCollins team: Susan Katz, Elise Howard, Kate Jackson, Diane Naughton, Cristina Gilbert, and Laura Kaplan. You've made this experience a pleasure as always.

Kate Lee, words can't express the gratitude I have for all the work you've done on my behalf. It's such a pleasure to work with you.

To my family: Mom, Dad, Adrianne, Erica, Marcus, Lisa, and William—thank you all for being there for me and supporting me through this process. I couldn't do it without you!

To all of my dear friends: Thank you for keeping me sane and sharing your passion for my books with your friends and family.

To my amazing staff: Laura, Kelly, Ashley, and Meghan, thank you for all that you do—and all the laughs!

Finally, to all of the teachers and librarians who love these books and invite me into your schools, I give you the greatest thanks.

Read on for a sneak peek at Mackenzie's next adventure!

Mixed Messages

Bluetopia

"I am soooo happy to have electricity and cell phones again," Mackenzie Blue Carmichael said to her friends.

"And warm showers," Zee's BFF, Ally Stern, agreed, sucking a Mocha Chiller through a straw.

"I don't know," Chloe Lawrence-Johnson replied in her southern accent. "I kind of miss being in the wilderness."

"Oh, I didn't mind being in the wilderness," Zee said. "I just don't think all the bugs and dirt needed to be there, too." She brushed off her red kimono tunic as if she were flicking away invisible grime.

"Isn't that kind of the point?" Jasper Chapman asked. "Don't bugs and dirt go with the wilderness?"

The four friends were sitting on the patio of the Brookdale Mall Café, reminiscing about their seventh-grade science field trip on Brookdale Mountain.

"All I'm saying is, I hope the eighth-grade field trip is to a spa," Zee explained.

"No, you don't." Chloe laughed. "Admit it. You had a great time."

Ally leaned closer to Zee and flashed a smile. "After all, I got to be there." Ally was visiting from Paris, where she had moved over the summer. She and Zee had been BFFs since before kindergarten and missed each other tons now that they lived so far apart. When Ally surprised Zee with a visit the week before, Zee was so excited to have all her friends together.

Zee rolled her eyes. "Okay, I had fun. But don't tell my parents. They're threatening to take Adam and me camping in the spring."

"I bet it would be awesome to go camping with your brother," Chloe said.

Zee shrugged. "Well . . . I don't know about that, but Adam's not really the problem. I think I might spontaneously combust if I ever have to go a week without the internet again."

"That would certainly be messy," Jasper said.

"Even without cell phones and the internet, I thought the week went by incredibly fast," Ally said.

"I hope this week doesn't," Zee told her. "You have to go back to Paris on Saturday."

"Don't remind me," Ally said, frowning. "I'm going to miss you so much." She turned to Jasper and Chloe. "You guys, too."

"I can't believe I'm going to have to say good-bye all over again," Zee said. "I'm going to be way sad."

"At least you'll still be able to IM and email," Chloe pointed out. Her green eyes sparkled with encouragement.

"I guess," Zee said with a sigh, "but it's not the same. Paris and California are in totally different time zones. So when I'm just getting to school, Ally's day is almost over."

"And by the time Zee gets home from school, it's usually time for me to go to sleep," Ally put in.

"When we finally do connect, we have to spend so much time catching up on what our friends did and said," Zee explained.

"And then we are usually interrupted before we get to the juicy stuff."

"It would be so much easier if we could just start with that," Zee added.

"Like you can on Facebook and MySpace?" Chloe said.

"What do you mean?" Zee asked.

"You can post pictures and updates and other information about yourself," Chloe said.

"Right!" Zee agreed. "Adam is constantly posting what he's doing every minute of every day—as if anyone cares."

"We wouldn't have to spend a lot of time filling one another in when we finally do chat," Ally said. "Our posts would keep our friends up-to-date, and they could read them whenever they wanted."

"You know so much about it, Chloe," Zee said. "Do you have a Facebook page?"

Chloe shook her head so fast, her thick ponytail nearly whipped her face. "No way! My parents won't let me join Facebook or MySpace until I'm older."

"I think my parents would," Ally said, looking hopefully at Zee.

"Count me out," Zee told her, and her shoulders slumped. "I already asked. Facebook rules say you have to be fourteen to have an account, and my parents love to follow rules."

"Those big sites make my mum nervous," Jasper put in matter-of-factly. "That's why I'm building my own social networking site for my friends back in England." Jasper had recently moved to Brookdale from London over the summer.

"*Excuse* me," Chloe said, putting down her strawberry-kiwi vitamin water. "You're *making* a site like that?"

"Well . . . yes," Jasper said.

"Cool beans!" Zee cheered. "But how come you never told us you were into computers?"

"I suppose because you never asked," Jasper answered. "And I didn't think it was important."

"It is soooo important," Zee said.

Ally nodded. "Yeah, very."

"Why?" Jasper asked.

"Because we're your best friends, and it's like you're keeping a major secret from us," Zee explained.

Jasper turned to Chloe with pleading eyes. Behind his round wire-rimmed glasses, they looked as though they were screaming, "Save me!"

"Don't look at me," Chloe protested. "I can't believe we didn't know."

"That's not how it works with my mates in England," Jasper said.

"It's because they're boys," Chloe said. "Girls share everything."

"Yeah, if you're going to hang out with us," Ally began, "you have to, too."

"Fine." Jasper threw his arms in the air, nearly knocking

over his half-full glass of milk. "I'm almost finished building the site. It's going to be by invitation only." Zee, Ally, and Chloe stared expectantly at him. "Of course, you three will be invited."

"Awesome!" Chloe cheered. "We finally get to meet your British friends!"

"I love the idea," Zee said. "Can I help you come up with stuff to put on it—stuff girls might like, too?"

"Sure! I was thinking about calling it Bluetopia anyway," Jasper blurted out.

"Bluetopia?" Zee could feel her face redden.

"As in *Mackenzie* Blue?" Ally asked.

Jasper shook his head slightly as if he hadn't realized he'd actually said the name out loud. "Uh . . . yeah," he stammered, looking down. "You know, because you're going to help, and I don't want to take all the credit."

"Jasper definitely doesn't like to be the center of attention the way that Zee does!" Chloe jumped in.

"Hey! What's that supposed to mean?" Zee laughed.

"You know what I mean," Chloe said. "You want to be a rock star. Jasper would rather be . . . a . . . a . . ."

"Yes?" Jasper prompted. "Go on."

"You know . . . a thing that's *not* shiny and bright and gets a lot of attention."

Jasper tugged at the collar of his green polo shirt. "A rock?"

"Uh . . . lemme get back to you on that," Chloe said. Then she turned to Zee and squeaked, "Help!"

Zee sucked the last drop of Mocha Chiller through her straw. "I've gotta get back home," she said. "My mom says I have to clean my room before our spa appointment at Wink! today."

Ally laughed. "Ginny said she's never seen anyone who can turn a spotless room into a demolition zone in less than twenty-four hours," she told Jasper and Chloe.

"I had some help getting it messy," Zee said, looking sideways at her friend.

"I'll help you clean it up," Ally said.

"And I will work on the code for the site," Jasper said.

The group got up from their table and headed to the bike rack. They unlocked their bikes and began to climb on as a gray minivan pulled up to the curb. It had barely stopped when the door slid open.

"You're not leaving, are you?" Conrad Mitori called to Zee and her friends as he stepped onto the sidewalk.

Marcus Montgomery landed next to him. "Hang out with us for a while," he said. Conrad and Marcus were also Brookdale Academy seventh graders.

Zee looked at Chloe. Chloe had a crush on Marcus, and Zee could tell that Chloe would have liked to stay longer. "Sorry, guys. We have to go home. We're getting manicures later," Zee explained.

"You're choosing manicures over us?" Marcus protested. He slapped his hand on his chest and staggered as though he'd just been wounded.

Conrad flapped his hands. "Well, we know how important it is to have perfect nails," he teased. "Not!"

Zee laughed. "Stop it, you g—" She paused when she saw Landon Beck, the boy who she had had a huge crush on since forever, come out of the van, too.

"Hi!" Landon said, staring right at Zee.

"Oh . . . uh . . . hi . . ." Zee stammered. "What's up?"

Landon shoved his hands in the pockets of his shorts and shrugged. "Not much," he said.

"Umm . . . are you going to hang out at the mall?" Zee asked.

Landon nodded so that his blond bangs bounced against his tan forehead. "Yeah," he said. Zee felt like fireworks were going off in her head, but Landon looked so calm. "You want to hang with us?"

"I can't," Zee said.

"Oh, okay."

Think of something to say, Zee told herself. *Anything.*

Luckily, Ally saved Zee. "You know, manicures aren't just for girls," she told Marcus and Conrad. "You guys could probably use one after a week in the woods."

"Are you getting one, Jasper?" Marcus asked.

"Oh no," Jasper said quickly. "The girls are on their own."

Conrad put his arm around Jasper. "So stick with us."

"I'm afraid I have to decline," Jasper said. "There's something I have to work on at home." He climbed onto his bike.

"Are you heading off to save a rain forest?" Conrad asked.

"Or planting one?" Marcus joked. Jasper spent a lot of time on environmental issues at Brookdale Academy. Along with Chloe, he had created a garden on campus where they could grow vegetables for the cafeteria, then turn the food scraps into compost for the plant beds.

"No, it has nothing to do with the environment," Jasper explained as he waved good-bye.

Conrad turned to Marcus and shrugged. "I thought everything he did had something to do with the environment."

Ally began to pedal away, too. "Good-bye."

"Later!" Marcus shouted.

Zee looked at Landon. "Bye," she said.

Landon smiled. "See ya!"

Zee's bike started to wobble. She straightened it up and followed her friends, quietly hoping that she could make it out of the boys' sight without doing something klutzy like falling off.

"Well . . . that was interesting," Ally said as they headed away from the mall.

"Very," Chloe agreed.

"What?" Zee asked.

"You know . . . Landon," Ally explained.

Zee stared at her friends sternly, hoping they'd get the message. Zee hadn't ever told Jasper that she had a crush on Landon.

Chloe didn't pick up on the hint. "As if you didn't know," Chloe said.

"Didn't know what?" Jasper asked.

"It's nothing," Zee quickly jumped in. Her red extra-high Converse sneakers pushed faster on the bike's pedals. This didn't feel like the time to spill the news about her crush to Jasper. "It was just interesting to see all the guys there."

Hi, Diary,

I can't believe that Landon actually wanted to hang with ME at the mall. ☺ At first, I was kind of worried because he wasn't acting like he wanted to talk to me. Then I realized—duh!—he was probably as nervous as I was. Will I ever stop feeling so scared around him?

But I've got bigger issues to deal with than Landon. I've got only one more week with Ally. Which means that all my best friends have only one more week together to get Bluetopia going. So the two most important things right now are:

1. Friends (Ally, Chloe, and Jasper)
2. Bluetopia

Landon can wait. He has to.

B-Z Zee

Tina Wells founded Buzz Marketing Group at the tender age of sixteen. She's spent the last decade keeping her finger on the pulse of what's hot for tweens and teens. Prior to becoming America's youth expert, she earned a B.A. in Communication Arts from Hood College, and she's currently a student at Wharton School of Business. Tina's many honors include *Essence* magazine's 40 Under 40 Award, *Billboard*'s 30 Under 30 Award, AOL Black Voices Black Women Leaders in Business top ten list, and the 2009 Entrepreneur of the Year Award from the Philadelphia Chamber of Commerce. She was also named one of Inc. com's Top 30 Entrepreneurs Under 30 and one of *Cosmopolitan*'s "Fun Fearless Phenoms." Tina serves on the boards of Friends of the Orphans and the Philadelphia Orchestra. She resides in southern New Jersey with her vast collection of shoes.